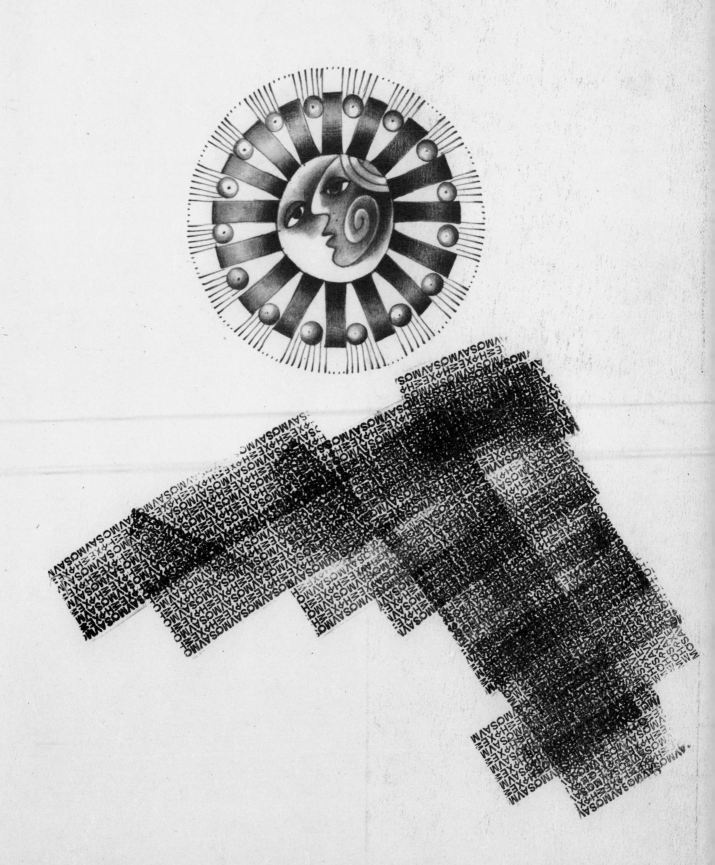

Folk Tales from India

FOLK TALES FROM INDIA

Retold by Vladimír Miltner
Illustrated by Vladimír Tesař

Hamlyn

LONDON · NEW YORK · SYDNEY · TORONTO

This edition first published 1978 by
The Hamlyn Publishing Group Limited
Translated by Inka Vostřezová
Graphic design by Bohuslav Blažej
Designed and produced by Artia for the Hamlyn Publishing Group Limited
London · New York · Sydney · Toronto
Astronaut House, Feltham, Middlesex, England
This edition © Artia 1978
Illustrations © Vladimír Tesař
ISBN 0 600 34901 2
Printed in Czechoslovakia by PZ Bratislava
1/01/30-51

CONTENTS

The sun shone down brilliantly out of a clear blue sky. Everything was quiet except for a slight quivering of the air above the stony downs, covered with sparse grass and dry trees. Up the dusty winding path came the wanderer, wearing a white dhoti, a long strip of cotton cloth wrapped round his skinny thighs and loins. He carried a simple stringed instrument, the iktar, and a small bundle containing all his belongings.

The wanderer scanned the countryside, took a deep breath of warm air, and said to himself: 'Yes, this is my India, my wonderful country, full of many scents and odours, parched and dusty for most of the year and washed by torrents of water during the remaining months; rich with immense treasures hidden deep in the earth and poor with the poverty of its innumerable inhabitants; great with its glorious past and miserably undeveloped and deprived of worldly goods; wise in its philosophy and foolish in its superstition...'

He followed the path and by sunset came to a village called Alandi. 'Jagannath is here!' cried a girl drawing water from a well by the village. 'Jagannath is here!' came the echo from the mud huts, across the village green and all around. Everyone, old and young, came to greet their good old friend, Jagannath.

Jagannath was a wandering story-teller. He was well known everywhere and everyone looked forward to his visits. Nobody knew where he came from or how old he was. Even the oldest villagers claimed that Jagannath used to tell them stories when they were little children.

Jagannath answered their greetings with a smile and headed for the bank of the river Indrayani, where he washed off the weariness of the long journey. Then he sat down under a spreading fig-tree and ate what the grateful villagers gave him: fried dough-cakes, wheat pan-cakes, cooked beans, ground peanuts flavoured with salt and red pepper, a glass of yoghurt, sugar-cane syrup, and a big peeled onion.

When the villagers had done their farm work and fed the cattle, they all sat down under the fig-tree Dabamba and Jagannath began telling a story.

Of the Adventurous King Vikram

Once upon a time in Ujjayini there ruled a very peace-loving and god-fearing old king. When he was about to die he had a splendid temple built in the jungle not far from the city and dedicated it to the god of wisdom, Ganesha. It was a marvellous temple, and the luxurious growth of the flowering trees, bushes and lianas surrounding it only emphasised its beauty. In the centre of the temple stood a great statue of Ganesha, resplendent in pure gold. Surrounding it were tall columns, each of which was decorated from top to bottom with scenes from the lives of the gods, demi-gods and holy men. The cupola on the tower was adorned with innumerable statues and at the top of the tower fluttered triangular pennants. Dozens of priests and holy men dwelt in the huts around the temple.

But when the old king died, leaving behind him the young prince

Vikramaditya, who was called Vikram for short, the priests and holy men left and the temple fell into decay until the jungle swallowed it up.

Meanwhile the king's good and faithful counsellor ruled the land as regent, and his son Bhatti became Vikram's best friend. The boys were of the same age, but Bhatti was more prudent and often had to curb the recklessness of the prince who flung himself into dangerous games and amusements.

A few years later Prince Vikram came of age and replaced the old counsellor, who had meanwhile passed away peacefully, with his son Bhatti. Vikram ruled the kingdom well, and was known far and wide for his generosity and fairness. But his longing for adventure never left him and it was well that he kept close to him the calm and prudent Bhatti.

One day Bhatti remembered the forsaken temple in the jungle and suggested to Vikram that in memory of the old king he should restore its past glory. Vikram fancied the idea and immediately sent woodcutters to cut down the dense forest surrounding it. The woodcutters were followed by carpenters, stone-masons, wood-carvers, sculptors and painters, and within a few days the temple regained its past splendour. And there stood the golden statue of Ganesha in all its beauty. King Vikram was so pleased with the temple that he and Bhatti often spent the night there. Once, after midnight, the dead king, Vikram's father, appeared to him and told him that beneath the richly branched brass incense stand a great treasure lay buried. Since the god Ganesha himself guarded it, it would be very difficult to obtain, but the king offered Vikram some advice. First, he must worship Ganesha for a long time and bring him offerings to avert his wrath and punishment. Then he must undergo a dangerous trial to find out whether Ganesha was convinced of the sincerity of his faith: he would have to jump from the tower onto the rough rocks below. If Ganesha was favourably inclined towards him, he would save him from death; if not, Vikram would perish.

In the morning Vikram told Bhatti about his strange dream and asked him for advice. Although Bhatti was on other occasions very cautious, this time he advised Vikram to undertake the task, but to avoid haste or rashness. And so King Vikram did honour to the god Ganesha and brought him rich offerings and presents and meditated on his wisdom and goodness.

Ganesha, the god with an elephant's head, is the son of Shiva, born of the goddess Parvati, Shiva's wife and daughter of the Himalayan mountains. Ganesha used to be a naughty little boy and once, when he had played an especially mischievous prank, his angry father boxed his ears. He must have been really infuriated, because he struck so hard that he knocked off his son's head and it rolled some distance away. 'Look what you've done,' cried his wife Parvati. 'Now hurry up and get the poor boy a new head. He can't stay like that!' And Shiva did as she said. He took the head of the first creature he met and quickly put it on Ganesha's body. It was an elephant's head. And since it can be assumed that in a big head there are plenty of brains, Ganesha became the god of wisdom, the patron of scholars, sages, swindlers, merchants, and all who need to use their brains in their work.

The days passed, but soon Bhatti decided it was time Vikram tried to get the treasure. Together they climbed to the top of the tower and the king fearlessly flung himself into the abyss. Suddenly Ganesha's golden statue ran out of the temple, caught the falling king in its arms, put him gently down on the floor, and returned to its place in the temple. This was the sign that Ganesha favoured Vikram. Meanwhile Bhatti had descended from the tower and both he and Vikram started digging under the brass incense stand. After digging six feet deep they came upon a casket covered with embossed ornaments, and when they opened it they gazed in astonishment. It was full of gold, diamonds, rubies, sapphires, emeralds, turquoises and pearls. A fortune of immense value! But King Vikram kept none of it for himself. He sold everything to goldsmiths and jewellers and gave the money to the poorest people in his kingdom. The only exception was one big emerald, which he gave as a present to Bhatti, but Bhatti said: 'Thank you, Your Majesty, my good friend, but I would like to ask a favour. Please do the same with this emerald as you have done with the rest of the treasure. I do not long for riches, because gold and jewels are not the most valuable things the wise should seek.' Vikram took back the emerald with a smile and thought: 'I have a wise counsellor.'

The two friends often slept in Ganesha's temple, as it was very pleasant and peaceful. The god Ganesha appeared to Vikram in his dreams and taught him wisdom and various skills. Ganesha took a liking to the just king and one day he said to him: 'You have gained enough wisdom for one mortal life. I shall not appear to you any more, but I will grant you one wish. What shall it be?' Vikram asked for a day to think the matter over and the next day stated his wish. His soul was to have the power of entering the bodies of those whose souls had left them, and while it dwelt there his own body was not to decay. Ganesha granted him this power, since he knew well that Vikram was wise enough not to abuse it.

But Kuput, the cunning son of the carpenter who had been curious to know what King Vikram and his counsellor did so often in Ganesha's temple, and so had followed them there, overheard the conversation. However, being a bit simple-minded he did not understand it fully and this proved to be his undoing later.

Next morning, King Vikram said to his counsellor and friend, Bhatti: 'The god Ganesha has granted me the power of letting my soul visit the bodies of the dead, while my own body awaits its return. I would like to try this out at once. What do you think?'

'That seems an excellent idea', replied Bhatti, 'but be careful not to make any mistakes, Your Majesty.'

They came out of the temple and saw a dead mynah bird lying in front of them. 'Look, Bhatti, this is just what I need. Please stay with my body and guard it until I return,' said Vikram. His soul entered the mynah bird's body and flew away. And this is what came to pass.

In a town on the banks of the river Tapti, there lived a rich merchant and his wife, and she was very friendly with the wife of their neighbour, a barber. The merchant did not approve of this friendship, because the barber's wife was a nasty spiteful woman, but his wife took no notice of him and did whatever she pleased. And so she soon became just as unpleasant or perhaps even worse than the barber's wife.

It was just at this time that King Vikram, changed into the mynah bird, came to the town. The merchant had just returned from a business journey and had brought beautiful fabrics from Benares and a charming slave-girl from Bengal, as presents for his king. The king was very pleased and in return gave the merchant a precious ring, which was of singular beauty and must have cost a fortune. When the merchant's wife saw the ring, she wanted to keep it, but the merchant just laughed at her. He hid the ring in a chest in his room and went to the tea-house for a chat with his friends.

His wife immediately called the barber's wife and told her about the ring. 'I'd like to see it,' said the barber's wife. 'Show it to me.'

'I can't,' replied the merchant's wife. 'My husband has hidden it in a chest in his room and has forbidden me to go there.'

'Don't be silly,' the barber's wife urged her. 'If he has gone to the tea-house to see his friends, he is not likely to return home soon. I won't tell him anything. Come on, show it to me!'

So, cautiously, they entered the merchant's room, opened the chest and behold! There was the ring which glittered with a dazzling radiance. 'Isn't it lovely!' said the barber's wife. 'If we took it and sold it, we'd have heaps of money, enough to buy dresses, jewellery, and ointments for the rest of our lives!'

'What do you mean?' said the merchant's wife indignantly. 'You wouldn't want to rob my husband, would you?'

'Why not?' retorted the barber's wife. 'He's stingy and mean to you, and he's so rich that he wouldn't be much the worse for the loss. The next time he returns from a journey he'll bring the king some more cloth and the king will give him another ring. I wouldn't hesitate. Let's sell the ring secretly and share the money.'

'No, we can't do that,' said the merchant's wife reluctantly. 'If we were found out, we would be severely punished. And the shame we'd bring on ourselves in the town!'

'Fiddlesticks!' cried the barber's wife. 'We're not so clumsy as to get caught doing it! And if there is no evidence nothing can happen to you.' And she took the ring. 'All right then,' agreed the merchant's wife. 'You keep it for the time being, and when it's convenient we'll sell it to the money-lender.' The barber's wife hid the ring in a knot she made at the edge of her gown and tiptoed away.

King Vikram, as the mynah bird, had been sitting on a branch near the window and watching all the time. He was curious to know how everything would turn out, and decided to pay close attention.

When the merchant came home in the evening, he wanted to enjoy a last look at the king's present before going to bed. But the ring was gone. He had no doubt that his wife had had a hand in the business. Infuriated, he pulled her out of bed and tied her to a post with strong hempen rope. 'Where did you put the ring, you unworthy hag?' he cried at her. 'If you don't give it back to me at once, I'll leave you tied up here all night and in the morning I'll have the guards take you to the Justice!' But his wife would not confess, and the merchant, tired of shouting at her, went to bed.

A moment later the barber's wife slipped in, quietly untied the merchant's wife, and let herself be tied up in her place. She said to her: 'Take the ring and hide it well somewhere. I'm afraid they might find it if we keep it at home.' The merchant's wife took the ring and began running from the house, but the merchant caught a glimpse of her through the window and taking her to be the thief, called to the servant: 'Come with me quickly, there's the thief! Hurry up, let's catch him!'

The merchant's wife ran as fast as her legs would carry her to the banks of the river Tapti, the merchant and his servant following at her heels. When she realised she could not escape, she climbed to the top of a spreading fig-tree, hoping they would not find her there. The merchant and the servant stopped just beneath it and looked all around for the vanished thief. The moon glimmered like a fish's eye but they found no trace of the thief. The servant suggested: 'Master, I shall climb up that fig-tree. He may be hiding in the branches.'

'All right,' said the merchant, 'go ahead.' The merchant's wife felt her blood turn cold with fright. But then she had a sudden idea. When the servant had almost reached her she whispered to him: 'Come closer to me, dear boy, come to me! You're the one I have always loved, not that idle husband of mine. Come up and kiss me!'

The servant climbed up and kissed her, but the merchant's wife bit off his tongue and he was in such pain that he fell out of the tree. He shrieked and moaned, pointing upwards and saying: 'Blahblah, blahblahblah!' The merchant, thinking he had seen a ghost in the tree, took fright and ran home as fast as he could. The servant ran behind him, calling 'blahblahblah!'

They arrived home out of breath and in the darkness the merchant did not recognise the barber's wife tied to the post. Thinking it was his own wife he started shouting: 'You villainous ape, disgrace to the family! Because of you I almost fell into the clutches of a ghost! You ought to be ashamed of yourself, you wretch!' Receiving no reply, he took a knife and cut off her nose. Then he went to bed.

Meanwhile the merchant's wife slipped the ring onto a twig, climbed down the fig-tree, and sneaked back home. The barber's wife greeted her angrily, whispering: 'Look what's become of me! That brute of yours has cut off my nose!' And she held it out mournfully.

'Never mind,' the merchant's wife consoled her. 'Tie me to the pole again and go home. Everything will turn out well.' The barber's wife tied her up and went away. Morning came and the merchant woke up. He wanted to call the guards and have them take his wife to the Justice, but as soon as his wife saw him she began to lament: 'Lord Almighty, what injustice I have to suffer! My husband suspects me of terrible deeds and I have done none of them! Lord, if I am innocent of the theft of the ring, please make my nose, which my brutal husband has cut off so unjustly, please make my pretty nose grow again!'

The merchant could not believe his ears, and when he came to the post he could not believe his eyes either — his wife's nose was back in its place!

Meanwhile, in the neighbouring house the barber was getting ready for work, and when his wife came home he called to her, 'Hand me my razor!' Deliberately she threw it down at his feet. The barber, enraged by her lack of respect, picked it up, and flung it back at her. At this his wife began to wail loudly: 'Help! Help! The scoundrel has thrown his razor at me and cut off my nose!'

The guards rushed to the house, tied up the innocent barber, and dragged him to the Justice, who condemned the poor man to be impaled on a stake. But just then King Vikram, who in the shape of the mynah bird had seen everything, flew to the Justice and said: 'Sir, be just. I know how it all came about.' And he told the Justice the whole truth. Later the ring was found on the fig-tree on the bank of the river Tapti, and that was sufficient evidence. The Justice set the barber free, and ordered the faithless wives to be whipped and driven out of the country. From then on the merchant and the barber spent many a happy hour at the tea-house.

King Vikram, having saved the innocent barber from cruel punishment and the merchant from the loss of his ring, flew back to Ganesha's temple and entered his own body. He embraced Bhatti and told him the whole story. 'It's unusually interesting,' he said, 'to take a look at the world through other than human eyes. I like it.'

Soon afterwards he informed Bhatti that he would once again go and seek adventure in some other creature's body. In order that the people of his city should not notice the king's long absence, Bhatti made it known that the king was ill. But Kuput, the carpenter's son, who found out that the king's illness was feigned, and that the king

would change into another creature, decided to profit from the situation. As soon as the king left, Kuput would seize his body and take his place as king.

Neither Vikram nor Bhatti suspected anything. King Vikram entered the body of a monkey, whose corpse he had come upon during a ride in the woods, and left the city. However, the moment he had gone, his body came alive, arousing Bhatti's suspicion. He didn't believe it was really King Vikram, since the king had only just left and intended to roam about for some time. He decided to put him to the test, and ordered the cook to serve plain and poorly flavoured food of the kind ordinary people eat. His suspicion was confirmed, for the false king enjoyed his meals, and had no complaints. No wonder, after all, since he was a carpenter's son. Bhatti knew he was an impostor, but for the time being could do nothing about it. And the carpenter's son could not return to his own body, as it had decayed in the meantime. The whole affair was a pretty mess...

Meanwhile, King Vikram, now a sturdy monkey, had joined a troop of monkeys living in the royal palace gardens of the neighbouring kingdom. The monkeys led a contented life there. The little prince used to play with them and they were fed with many choice morsels and titbits from the royal kitchen. The king also kept a large flock of sheep and rams. One of these rams had a sweet tooth and during the night would steal into the kitchen and devour everything it could find. The cooks would beat it and fling things at it, all in vain: the ram's appetite could not be curbed. When Vikram realised this he spoke to the monkeys: 'Brothers and sisters, that gluttonous ram which devours everything it finds will soon be the cause of our downfall. The only way we can save ourselves is by leaving these royal gardens and moving deep into the jungle.'

The monkeys looked at each other in astonishment, made rude gestures, and said: 'How could a gluttonous ram, which is always poking its nose into the kitchen, be the downfall of us harmless monkeys? What connection is there between us and him, clever?'

'Don't you see?' replied Vikram. 'Well then, I'll explain. The cooks fling anything they happen to have with them at the ram. It may happen one day that in their anger they will throw a burning log. His fleece will catch fire and in confusion he'll run to the stable, which is full of straw. He will set the stable on fire, and all the king's horses — the blacks, the whites, the greys and the bays — will be badly burned. King Chandra will want to have them healed. He will call the veterinary surgeon who will inform him that the best way to cure horses' burns is with monkey lard. Then we are sure to die, as the king loves his horses much better than he loves us.'

The monkeys laughed at the idea, some covertly, others openly, and said: 'You nitwit, you idiot, have you gone out of your mind? Do you think we'd leave this place, where we are fed so well, and return to the jungle to eat wild fruits, small and tasteless and making our mouths sour? Never!'

King Vikram answered sadly: 'Alas! You will not listen to the voice of reason. I'm sorry to lose you, my monkey friends. I shall go to the jungle alone and you can stay here and enjoy your dubious dainties. I don't want to see the destruction of your tribe.' And alone he went deep into the jungle.

A few days later it came to pass as Vikram had foreseen. The ram stole into the kitchen again and sneaked around. The enraged cook picked up a burning log and hit it on the back. The ram's fleece caught fire and, bleating with pain, it ran to the stable where it rolled in the straw. The straw flared up and suddenly the whole stable was in flames. Many of the horses were burnt to death, others suffered terrible burns. King Chandra, horrified and desolate at the injury to his beloved horses, called the veterinary surgeon and asked: 'What, sir, is the best remedy for these terrible burns?'

The veterinary surgeon stroked his beard for a while and then replied: 'There are many healing balms, oh king! But the best and unique remedy is certainly monkey lard.'

No sooner had the king heard this, than he ordered his soldiers to kill all the monkeys in the royal gardens and to bring their lard to the surgeon. The whole monkey tribe was destroyed. Vikram did not witness the destruction with his own eyes. He was deep in the jungle, but rumour of this terrible event reached his ears because all the animals talked about it in horror. He said to himself: 'I will not suffer this injustice! I must avenge the monkeys and punish cruel King Chandra.'

One day, as he was wandering through the jungle, he came to a beautiful pond covered with white, blue and pink water-lilies. He was very thirsty and was about to take a drink of water when he noticed there were footprints leading into the pond but none leading out. 'There must be a demon in this pond! I'll have to drink carefully and from afar so that he can't do me any harm,' he thought. He broke off a reed and standing far away from the water's edge, he sucked the water through it. Just as he finished drinking, the surface of the water broke into waves and a hideous demon came up in the centre of the pool. He was wearing a necklace of precious stones. With a terrifying laugh he said to Vikram: 'I am the all-devouring demon, Shunga. Whosoever enters my pool shall be devoured by me. But I have never yet met with as cunning a creature as you are, monkey, sucking water through a reed. I admire you for that. Therefore tell me your wish and I shall grant it to you.'

'Since you are a devouring demon,' said Vikram, 'tell me how much you can manage to devour.'

'I can manage to devour hundreds, thousands, even hundreds of thousands of those who step into the water. But on dry land I'm so weak that even a tiny puppy could overcome me.'

'Well, Shunga, give me your necklace of precious stones and I will bring all King Chandra's courtiers to your pool,' said the monkey. Shunga gave him the necklace and Vikram returned to the city. He put on the necklace and leaped around among the trees of the royal gardens. When the courtiers saw him, they called at him in wonder:

'Hey, monkey! Where did you get that lovely necklace of precious stones that glitter so brightly?'

And Vikram replied: 'There is a pool of the god of treasures hidden in the jungle. Whosoever enters it when the sun has half-risen above the horizon will emerge with a necklace like this one.'

King Chandra soon heard the news and summoned Vikram to come before him. He asked: 'Is what you told my courtiers, and what they told me, true?'

'Certainly, oh king! This necklace which you see round my neck proves it,' answered Vikram.

King Chandra, possessed by greed, said urgently: 'I'll go there with all my courtiers and we can all have a necklace like yours. Tomorrow morning you must take us there.' And so Vikram did.

At sunrise, when they came to the pool, Vikram the monkey said to the King Chandra: 'Let the courtiers go into the pool first, oh king! Then I'll tell you something important.' The courtiers disappeared into the pool and there the demon Shunga devoured them all. Vikram, the monkey, quickly climbed a tall tree and from the top called to the lone King Chandra: 'Oh, you cruellest of kings! You shall never live to see your courtiers again! They have all been eaten up by the devouring demon Shunga, who dwells in this pond. Now I have avenged the monkey tribe that used to live in your gardens, the tribe you so wantonly destroyed.'

Then King Chandra bowed his head in shame and walked away sadly. Vikram, having avenged the dead monkeys, returned to Ujjayini. But the carpenter's son, Kuput, still dwelt in his body, so King Vikram had to remain a monkey. Bhatti pondered in vain how to oust Kuput from the royal body, until at last he hit on a good plan. He arranged for a ram-fight to be held, because Kuput had a passion for gambling and always played his ram for high stakes. Bhatti was well aware of this and so in good time he had a very strong ram sent from Kashmir. As soon as the fight began it was obvious that the Kashmir ram would win. False King Kuput clenched his fists and ground his teeth, but the next time the rams butted each other his ram fell dead. So as not to lose the bet, Kuput quickly entered its body and charged at the Kashmir ram. King Vikram did not wait, but promptly acquired his own body. Then Bhatti drew a sword and cut off the Kuput-ram's head. And so Vikram returned to his own body and ruled again.

On the square in front of the royal palace in Ujjayini there used to be a little shop. The owner sold all sorts of sweetmeats: nuts, almonds, sultanas, dried fruit, but above all, various kinds of betel rolls, which he would prepare in the customer's presence according to his wishes. He would take a bright green betel leaf, spread fine lime on it, add nuts, spices and other tasty things, roll up the leaf and pin it up with a piece of clove. Then he would hand the roll to the customer, happy to hear him praise what he had produced.

A beautiful maiden, exquisitely dressed and adorned with jewels of immense value, used to visit the shop every day. No one knew her. She would buy a single betel roll, and having given the shopkeeper a whole gold coin, she would leave in silence. She never bargained, never said a word, just took the betel roll, put the coin on the counter and went.

The shopkeeper often puzzled over this, but could come to no conclusion. One day he mentioned the mysterious maiden to his friend, King Vikram's priest, who offered sacrifices to the gods for the king. The priest, inquisitive as most priests are, decided to solve the mystery. The next day he loitered about the square and when the maiden, as usual, bought her betel roll and was walking off, he secretly followed her.

The maiden left the city and headed for a wooded mountain. At the top of the mountain, there was a dark cavern. The maiden entered the cavern and vanished.

The priest, hesitating at first, decided to follow her. Cautiously, he stepped inside the cavern and walked on and on. All at once the rocks in front of him parted and the astonished priest beheld a marvellous land with a big city, in the centre of which was a beautiful park. In this park stood a golden castle. 'What a lovely city!' thought the priest. 'I must find out who reigns here.' And he headed straight for the castle.

When he came to the park he saw the maiden he had been following, among many other maidens, all looking like her. He approached them with a greeting. The maidens bowed slightly, but said nothing.

'Who are you, and who reigns over this city?' asked the priest. One of the maidens answered: 'Our Queen Abol-rani reigns here, and we are her followers. But our queen is displeased when strangers intrude on us. You had better return where you came from, holy man.'

'I don't fancy that,' said the priest audaciously. 'I'd like to meet your queen and pay my respects to her.'

'Our queen doesn't want to meet anyone,' said the maiden. 'She lives behind four curtains, secluded from the world, receiving no one.'

But the priest retorted: 'I will not leave this place until I have seen Queen Abol-rani!'

'Well then,' said the maiden, smiling, 'since you insist on meeting our queen, first come and bathe in this pond.' And the maidens surrounded the priest, and led him to a pond full of thousands of water-lilies all abloom in glorious colours.

But no sooner had he touched the water than he felt everything spin, his sight was dimmed and in a moment he found himself standing on the square in Ujjayini, in front of the shop where betel rolls and other sweetmeats were sold. The shop was closed and the square was empty. It was exactly midnight. The priest couldn't believe what had happened to him. Confused, he went home and to bed. But he could not sleep and tossed about in bed until daybreak.

In the morning he hurried to King Vikram, and described everything he had experienced in detail. The king was very interested and when the priest concluded his description, he ordered: 'You must come and show me where the cavern is, right away!' And they went.

At the top of the mountain King Vikram entered the cavern, and the priest returned to Ujjayini. The king walked boldly on and on, until the rocks before him parted and he beheld Queen Abol-rani's city. He headed resolutely towards the golden castle.

In the park in front of the castle the queen's maidens were making wreaths of flowers. King Vikram approached them with a greeting and asked: 'Who are you, and who reigns over this city?' The maidens bowed slightly, saying nothing.

'We are of the retinue of Queen Abol-rani,' answered one of the maidens. 'She reigns here.'

'I am King Vikramaditya of Ujjayini and I would like to meet your queen.'

The maidens exchanged smiles and one of them said: 'Come then, but first you must bathe in this pool.'

King Vikram laughed and said firmly: 'I don't mean to return to Ujjayini in any strange way. I want to meet Queen Abol-rani first, and then I shall bathe in the pool if you wish.' The maidens were surprised that the king had seen through their pretence, and said: 'We shall announce you to the queen. Should she be willing to receive you, she will do so. But she lives behind four curtains, so you won't see her anyway.'

'We'll see,' laughed the king and the maidens left to announce the visitor to Queen Abol-rani. A moment later they came back and one of them said: 'You may enter. The queen will receive you. But she never speaks to men. And since you won't even get a glimpse of her behind the curtains, I can't imagine why you insist on being received.'

'That's my own affair,' said King Vikram and, followed by the maidens, he entered the golden castle. But the maiden replied: 'No doubt; but you will need all your wisdom and courage. If you can make all four curtains drop away before sunset, you will behold our queen, and she will speak to you. But if you do not succeed, you will die!'

They entered a magnificent hall with a floor made of eight rare kinds of wood, walls lined with precious stones, and a crystal ceiling. Behind four curtains, each of which was embroidered in different colours and designs, seated on a soft couch of leopard skins, was Queen Abol-rani. But King Vikram could not see her. The maidens beckoned him to be seated and sat down around him.

'Hail, Queen Abol-rani,' said King Vikram. 'I have come from Ujjayini to meet you and I thank you for receiving me.' The curtains swayed slightly, but the queen didn't utter a word. 'Well,' said King Vikram, 'since the queen will not answer me perhaps her ear-rings will answer instead.' The maidens laughed merrily at the idea, but to their surprise the queen's ear-rings jingled and answered: 'We are listening, oh king, and will answer you!'

'I will tell you a story, then,' said King Vikram, and began...

In a certain village there lived four youths, all good friends. The first was of the rank of priests, the second of the rank of warriors, the third of the rank of merchants, and the fourth of the rank of workmen. They decided to go out into the world and learn a trade. They bade farewell to their parents and relatives and left.

Towards evening they came to a village and there asked a wood-carver to give them shelter for the night. In the morning, when they were about to set out on their journey again, the wood-carver offered to take one of them as an apprentice. The workman stayed with him, and the others went on their way.

That day, towards evening, they asked a weaver to give them shelter for the night. And again the weaver said he would take one of them as an apprentice. The merchant stayed with him. The following day only two of the friends continued their journey. In the evening, when they came to a village, they found lodgings at a goldsmith's. And the warrior stayed as his apprentice.

Then the priest's son walked on alone. In the evening he came to a hermitage in a wood, which was the dwelling of a holy man. And the holy man took him into apprenticeship.

So each of the friends found a master, and worked hard to learn his trade. After twelve years of study, the priest said goodbye to the holy man, and set out on his way home. He stopped at the goldsmith's for his friend, the warrior; together they stopped at the weaver's for the merchant; and all three of them went to the wood-carver for the workman. Together again, they headed for home.

Night befell them in a forest. They lay down on the soft grass and agreed to take turns in keeping watch. The first to keep watch was the workman, who had learnt the art of wood-carving. He became bored with watching, and in order not to fall asleep he took a big branch, and carved a wooden maiden from it. During the next watch, the merchant, who had learnt the art of weaving, wove a garment for her. The warrior-goldsmith made her ear-rings, bracelets, rings and a necklace, and when it came to the turn of the priest, who had studied with the holy man, he decided to endow her with life. He uttered a magic formula and the maiden opened her eyes and spoke.

Now the four friends began to quarrel about which of them she should belong to...

King Vikram came to the end of his tale, and added: 'Tell me, dear ear-rings, to whom should the maiden rightfully belong?'

The ear-rings jingled softly and said: 'The maiden rightfully belonged to him who endowed her with life.'

At that moment Queen Abol-rani, displeased with the answer, exclaimed: 'What foolish nonsense!' She tore off her ear-rings and flung them on the floor. 'You are not worthy of being worn by me! He who endowed her with life is like a god. He who made her is like a father. He who gave her a garment is like a brother and he who adorned her is her husband. The maiden rightfully belonged to the goldsmith!' No sooner had the queen spoken than the first curtain fell down, and only three more curtains hid her from Vikram's sight.

'Now I will tell you the second story,' continued King Vikram. 'If the queen will not answer me, perhaps her necklace will answer instead.' The queen's maidens laughed merrily, but the necklace jingled and said: 'I am listening, king, and I shall answer you!'

And King Vikram began...

In one town, there lived a merchant with his wife and son. After some time his wife bore him a daughter and they gave her the name Chandraprabha — Moonshine. When Chandraprabha grew up, she surpassed in beauty all the maidens in the whole kingdom. Suitors began to visit the merchant's house, asking his daughter's hand.

And so the merchant chose one of the suitors, a clever craftsman, who knew how to make a flying carriage and move around the sky in it as do the gods. On the same day, the merchant's wife, who knew nothing of her husband's arrangement, promised her daughter to a wise prophet, who knew of all things past, present and future. And their son, who had no suspicion of what his parents had done, promised his sister to a warrior of the Kshatra caste. When the merchant, his wife and his son met and discovered they had each promised Chandraprabha to a different suitor, they were very confused and at a loss.

On a day determined by the astrologers in accordance with the positions and movements of heavenly bodies and confirmed by their books, the three suitors — the craftsman, the prophet and the warrior — came to the merchant's house. But the charming Chandraprabha was gone. She had vanished mysteriously and no one had any notion where she was. They searched the house, the garden and the whole city, all in vain.

The desolate father turned to the sage: 'You are a prophet! Tell us where my daughter is!' The sage closed his eyes, pondered a while, and then said: 'The evil demon, Pishach, has carried away your daughter to his den in the Himalayan mountains.'

'Woe is me,' cried the merchant's wife. 'Never again shall I see my darling daughter!'

'Do not despair,' said the craftsman. 'I shall build a flying carriage, and we'll get there in the twinkling of an eye.' No sooner said than done. When the flying carriage was ready, the craftsman, the prophet and the warrior boarded it and flew off.

As soon as they arrived at the Himalayan mountains the evil

demon Pishach rushed out at them in rage. The warrior of the Kshatra caste fought him bravely. There followed a terrible battle, but it did not last long, since the warrior cracked the demon's skull with an arrow, the head of which was a hardened half-moon. Having rescued Chandraprabha, they all flew back.

Chandraprabha's parents and brother were happy to see her alive and well, but now they all began to argue about which of the three suitors should have the beautiful maiden...

King Vikram came to the end of the tale, and added: 'Tell me, dear necklace, which of the suitors did the maiden rightfully belong to?'

The necklace softly jingled and said: 'The maiden rightfully belonged to him who by the power of his spirit found out where the demon had hidden her.'

At that moment Queen Abol-rani, displeased with the answer, exclaimed: 'What foolish nonsense!' She tore off her necklace and flung it on the floor. 'You are not worthy of being worn by me! The maiden rightfully belonged to the warrior of the Kshatra caste! Risking his own life, he saved her by the vigour and strength of his arms. The prophet and the craftsman were only sent by fate to help him. Isn't that what prophets and craftsmen are here for?' And no sooner had the queen finished speaking than the second curtain fell down, and she was hidden from Vikram's sight only by two curtains.

'Now I shall tell you the third story,' said King Vikram. 'If the queen will not answer me, perhaps her bracelet will answer instead.' The queen's maidens laughed merrily but the bracelet jingled and replied: 'I am listening, oh king, and will answer you!'

And King Vikram began...

Once upon a time there was a kingdom, and in it lived a king and a queen. They were very sad, because they had no children. Often they would bring offerings and gifts to the goddess Parvati and pray that she would give them a son. And indeed, after some time the queen bore a son. They gave him the name Madhukar. The king and the queen were very happy, and in gratitude they continued to bring offerings to the goddess Parvati, and taught their son, Prince Madhukar, to do likewise. And so the prince, whenever he was passing a temple dedicated to the goddess in any of her divine forms, would enter the temple and sacrifice at least a handful of rice or a few flowers.

When Madhukar grew up, he married the daughter of the neighbouring king; her name was Kumudini. She was beautiful and kind, and Madhukar's aged father passed on the crown to his son. So Madhukar became king, and Kumudini queen.

One day, just before the spring holidays, Madhukar and Kumudini decided to visit Kumudini's parents. It was not very far to their royal seat and so the couple took a carriage, driven by Madhukar's best friend and counsellor. The thoroughbred horses set off at a fast trot.

On their way they passed a magnificent temple of the goddess Parvati. Madhukar told his counsellor to stop the horses, and then he stepped from the carriage. 'I will offer up some water-lilies to the goddess Parvati to whom I owe my life,' he said to his wife Kumudini. 'Wait for me here a little while...'

From a nearby pool he plucked an armful of the flowers and entered the temple. He offered the water-lilies to the goddess Parvati, and promised that on his way back he would make her another offering. Then he went back to the carriage and they all drove on.

When the spring holidays were over, Madhukar, his wife Kumudini and his counsellor, who drove the horses, bade farewell and set out on the return journey. As they came to the goddess Parvati's temple, King Madhukar stopped the carriage so he could offer an armful of water-lilies to the goddess. But the water-lilies had faded and not a single flower was to be found in the pool. Madhukar guiltily entered the temple, and prayed to the goddess, wondering what he should do all the while; he had nothing to sacrifice to her. Suddenly it occurred to him that the best way of honouring her would be to sacrifice his own life. Without thinking twice, he drew his sword and cut off his own head.

Queen Kumudini and the counsellor waited and waited, but King Madhukar did not arrive. After a while the counsellor said: 'My queen, please allow me to go to the king. Apparently he is in deep meditation and has forgotten the passing of time.' The queen gave him permission and the counsellor entered the temple. He was horrified to see there the dead king. His heart was full of sorrow at his friend's death and he felt deeply for the queen. How was he to tell her the terrible truth? So, in despair, he too drew his sword and cut off his own head.

The queen, impatiently waiting for her husband and the counsellor, got down from the carriage and decided to look inside the temple

herself. When she saw the two men, both dead, she began to weep. 'What is left for me in life? Nothing! It has no meaning for me. I shall offer up my life too.' She was about to kill herself with Madhukar's sword, when the goddess Parvati suddenly appeared in the temple and said in a kind voice: 'Stay your hand. Do not act rashly! Let there be no more human sacrifices! If you want to bring your husband and his counsellor back to life, take their heads and place them on their bodies.' And with that, the goddess disappeared.

Joyfully Queen Kumudini hurried to place the severed heads on the bodies. Instantly they grew together, and both men stood before the queen alive and well. But alas! In her hurry the queen had confused the heads and the bodies. She had placed her husband Madhukar's head on the counsellor's body and the counsellor's head on the king's body...

King Vikram concluded his story, and added: 'Tell me, bracelet, which of the two did the queen rightfully belong to?'

The bracelet softly jingled and said: 'The queen rightfully belonged to him who had the king's body, for the body is larger than the head.'

At that Queen Abol-rani, displeased with the answer, cried: 'What foolish nonsense!' She pulled off her bracelet and flung it on the floor. 'You are not worthy of being worn by me! The queen rightfully belonged to him who had the king's head! For the head is the most important of all the parts of the body; it carries a person's image and reason.' No sooner had the queen spoken than the third curtain fell to the floor, and only the last one now hid the queen from Vikram's sight.

'I will now tell you the fourth and last story,' continued King Vikram. 'If the queen will not answer me, perhaps her emerald ring will answer instead.' The queen's maidens did not laugh this time, because they had witnessed King Vikram's power and knew that, should he wish it, the emerald ring would answer. And indeed, the emerald ring glittered dark green and said: 'I am listening, oh king, and will answer you!'

And King Vikram began telling his story...

Once upon a time there was a kingdom in the south, ruled by a kind and just king. But wicked courtiers stirred up a rebellion, and the king with his queen and the princess had to flee from the country under cover of night. They came to a dark wood in the neighbouring kingdom and were at once attacked by the fierce Shabars, hunters who dwelt in those regions. The king fought them like a lion, killing a great number, but there were so many of them that he was overcome and himself killed in the end. The terrified queen and princess had taken shelter in the bushes. When the battle was over and the Shabars had left with their booty, they both hurried on, weeping and crying, and did not stop until they came to the distant banks of a lovely lake with thousands of water-lilies floating on its surface.

It happened that just at that time the king of the land and his son, who were out hunting, came to the wood. When they saw the footprints of the two fugitives, the king said to his son: 'Look, two ladies have gone that way. Let us follow them and then each of us can choose the one he likes.'

'I would prefer the one with the smaller footprints,' said the prince. 'Evidently she must be the younger one, and is therefore more suitable for me. You take the one with the larger footprints.' The king agreed and so they spurred on their horses and followed the footprints. After a while they reached the lake and there found the queen and the princess resting on the sandy shore.

Seeing the two horsemen, the queen sprang up in terror, taking them to be robbers. 'Let's run away, my dear,' she cried. But her daughter said: 'Don't be afraid, mother dear, those men are not robbers. They look like hunters and I think they may help us.' The king and his son had meanwhile come closer and dismounted from their horses, and the king addressed the two ladies: 'Who are you, resting here with no one to protect you? Where do you come from and where are you going?'

The unfortunate queen then told them everything.

'Well,' said the king, 'my son and I have just decided to marry you both. My wife died a long time ago and my son is still single. What do you think? Do you like us?'

The queen and the princess sat there coyly in silence, and with bowed heads. The prince hastened to add: 'And my father would like the one with the larger feet but I would marry the one with the smaller feet. My father and I agreed upon this when we were following your footprints.'

At this the princess laughed and said: 'That's an idea! My mother has smaller feet than I have! The king laughed too, and said: 'Indeed, ha, ha... but that's what we agreed upon and we shall not change our minds. Gentlemen never go back on their word.' He was glad that he was going to have a young wife, whereas his son would have to be content with her mother. The queen and the princess were both happy to get a new home, and after a little coy hesitation they consented. The prince had nothing to add. Some time later there was a glorious double wedding in the royal palace. And just imagine — the daughter became her mother's mother-in-law and the mother became her daughter's daughter-in-law. The son was his father's father-in-law, and his father was his son-in-law. And later, sons and daughters were born of both marriages...

King Vikram came to the end of his story, and added: 'Tell me, emerald ring, what is the relationship between the children who sprang from those marriages?'

The emerald ring once more glittered with dark green radiance, and said. 'I cannot answer that question, oh king. I do not know.'

At that Queen Abol-rani, content with the answer, cried: 'Yes, emerald ring, you are worthy of being worn by me! You are not ashamed to admit that you do not know the correct answer, when you really do not know it. For there is no clear answer in this case and therefore the question cannot be answered.'

No sooner had the queen spoken than the fourth and last curtain fell down, and the queen was revealed to Vikram in all her sublime beauty. She bowed to Vikram and said: 'Welcome to my castle, King Vikram! You are the first man to behold me with your own eyes. Be welcome, King Vikram!' She descended from her soft couch of leopard skins and kissed Vikram on the lips.

The king then took her to Ujjayini and married her. Together they lived a life of delight and joy, but the adventurous Vikram could not stay at home for long. One day, he let his spirit enter the body of a parrot and flew off to the jungle.

There, the parrots who admired his wisdom, his good ideas and the good advice he gave them, elected him chief of the parrots. They took his advice and obeyed him, and thus no misfortune befell them. Only once did they not heed him, and were almost caught in a hunter's net. At the last moment King Vikram managed to save them, but he himself could not escape.

'What will you do with me?' he asked the hunter.

'I shall sell you,' replied the hunter.

Vikram said: 'I'll tell you what to do. Take me to the town, Mau, and sell me to the merchant Baniya. He will give you a thousand gold coins for me.'

The hunter did not believe him: 'A thousand gold coins for one parrot? Impossible! No one has ever given me more than one gold coin!'

'Try it and you'll see,' said Vikram.

The hunter shook his head doubtfully, but nevertheless he went to Mau. There he found the merchant Baniya and offered him the parrot.

Tales Told by the Wanderer in Alandi

'How much do you want for it?' asked the merchant.

The hunter replied: 'A thousand gold coins and he's yours.'

The merchant, at first stupefied, then started to roar with laughter. 'You must be mad! For a thousand gold coins I could get an elephant, and a baby elephant into the bargain!'

At this point Vikram spoke. 'Do not be rash in your judgment, Baniya. Buy me at this price and you won't regret it. I will advise you in your business, and soon you will be the richest merchant in the whole kingdom.'

Baniya gave the hunter the thousand gold coins and Vikram stayed in Mau. Flying all over the district, he listened to the business dealings of other merchants, and was always on the look out for good bargains. He told Baniya everything he found out, and at the same time gave him good advice on what, when and how to do everything. Thanks to him, the merchant prospered greatly and within a single week he had doubled his fortune. 'You see I am worth the price you paid, Baniya,' said Vikram. 'I will make one more suggestion to help you keep your customers and gain many more. Each time you weigh a pound of rice add a few grains; each time you measure a length of cloth, add an inch; each time you pour a pint of milk add a few drops. You will be none the worse for it and the customers will come to you rather than go to the other merchants, who are more likely to give a little less of everything.' Merchant Baniya had by now found out that the parrot always advised him well, and so he accepted this suggestion.

There was a dancer named Champa-bai, who also lived in Mau. One day she heard what the woodcutter Lakarhar had told his friends. He had dreamt that he had married Champa-bai and as a wedding present had given her a thousand gold coins. When Champa-bai learned of this she ran to the Justice and accused Lakarhar: 'Yes, the rumour is true. We were married secretly, but Lakarhar has never given me a wedding present and I am going to sue him. I want him to give me a thousand gold coins!' The Justice summoned the woodcutter Lakarhar to court and questioned him on the matter.

Astounded, Lakarhar stated: 'It is not true. I am still single. I only dreamt of what Champa-bai has told you and I described my dream to my friends — that is all!'

'He is lying, sir, because he does not want to give me what he promised!' cried Champa-bai. The Justice was at a loss and did not know how to settle the case. Then he remembered Baniya's clever parrot and sent a servant for him. Parrot Vikram considered the main points of the argument and then he whispered something to the Justice. The Justice called a servant and in a low voice gave him an order. The servant left and after a while returned carrying a sealed pot.

Vikram turned to the greedy, lying dancer and said: 'There are a thousand gold coins in this pot — exactly the sum you demand. If you can manage to take them out of the pot without breaking the seal, they are yours.' Champa-bai rushed to the pot and tried to get the gold coins out of it, but she failed to do so. 'It can't be done,' she said in a disappointed voice. 'I would have to break either the seal or the pot.'

'You see,' said Vikram, 'just as you cannot get a thousand gold coins out of this sealed pot, you cannot get them from a poor woodcutter. How could anything so silly occur to you?' The judge was glad that the parrot had passed just judgment, but Champa-bai, who had been put to shame in front of the whole town, swore a terrible revenge on Vikram. Vikram discovered this and fluttering over her, said: 'Do not think of revenge, you foolish woman! You would lose everything you have and in the end die in disgrace!' But Champa-bai did not heed his warning.

Some time afterwards, Baniya's eldest son's wedding took place. Champa-bai danced at the sumptuous feast, which was attended by almost all the citizens of Mau. Her dancing was beautiful, for she had the grace of a fairy. Merchant Baniya, who was a bit drunk, said: 'As a reward for your beautiful dancing, choose whatever you wish to have from my house.'

'I want the parrot! Parrot Vikram!' exclaimed Champa-bai.

The merchant was at a loss, for he had not anticipated such a wish, but a promise is a promise and he had to give Champa-bai the parrot to whom he was obliged for his wealth. 'Don't be angry with me, parrot Vikram,' said merchant Baniya sadly. 'I am very sorry to have done such a foolish thing. Please forgive me and do not think badly of me.'

'Never mind, Baniya,' said Vikram. 'No one can escape his fate. And even though evil be plotted, it may turn into good if it so stands written in the book of Fate.'

When he had finished speaking, parrot Vikram said goodbye to merchant Baniya. He sat on Champa-bai's shoulder and let her take him to her house.

Champa-bai felt deep satisfaction at having the parrot in her power, and gloated over her impending revenge. She ordered the cook to bake the parrot for lunch. The only thing Vikram could do under the circumstances was to feign death. In vain he tried to find a way of escaping the dishonourable fate that was imminent. The cook took him to the kitchen and there she plucked off his feathers. When she turned away to prepare the pan with oil, Vikram hid in a garbage pit since, being featherless, he could not fly away. A moment later, the cook found that the parrot was gone. Terrified of what her mistress would do to her, she killed a chicken and served that instead of the parrot. First she served up the bird's head and the malicious Champa-bai ate it with great relish and satisfaction, without noticing that she had been deceived. Parrot Vikram had to hide in the pit until he had grown new feathers, feeding on remains of food that had been thrown away. When at last he was able to fly, he waited for a favourable opportunity and left the town for the jungle, where he hid behind the statue of the god Vishnu in a small temple. There he hoped to recover from the hardships he had endured.

It was to this very temple that Champa-bai used to go to pray to the god Vishnu, begging him to take her to heaven alive because she was afraid of death. Parrot Vikram heard her plea and, from behind Vishnu's statue, in a sublime, godly voice spoke thus: 'Yes, my child, so dear to the gods, you shall be granted what you deserve. Now go home, give away all you have to the poor of the town of Mau and burn down your house so that nothing remains of it. Come here on the day of the new moon and you will be taken to heaven.'

Champa-bai did as the parrot told her. Everyone in town was surprised by her sudden generosity to the poor, having always known her to be mean and stingy. Of course, Champa-bai made no secret of the favour the god Vishnu was about to bestow on her and so, on the day of the new moon a big crowd of people from the town and from far and wide, drawn by curiosity, gathered at the god Vishnu's temple.

First Champa-bai danced a ceremonial religious dance and then, bowing reverently to Vishnu, she said in a trembling voice: 'Lord, I have come because you have promised to take me to heaven alive so that I will not have to die, as ordinary human beings do. I am here, Vishnu, and am waiting.' The statue neither moved nor spoke. Nothing happened. The impatient dancer stamped her foot on the tiled floor of the temple. 'Well, I am here and am waiting, Vishnu!' But again, nothing happened. Laughter could be heard from the crowd of onlookers. Champa-bai, pale with anger, began to beat Vishnu's statue with her fists and shouted: 'Liar! Cheat! What about your promise?' Now the crowd roared with laughter.

Suddenly, parrot Vikram flew out of his hiding-place. A silence fell upon the crowd. When Champa-bai saw the parrot she thought she had eaten, she nearly fainted with fear and anguish. Vikram, hovering above Champa-bai, said: 'It was not Vishnu who spoke to you but I, to punish you for your bad deeds. One part of what I predicted has already come true — you are penniless. And if there is any justice, the other part of my prediction will come true as well.'

Humiliated and desperate, Champa-bai fell on the ground and furiously beat her head against a rock until she killed herself. Although she had been the best and most beautiful of dancers, no one pitied her, for she had been an evil woman too.

Vikram was tired of his adventurous way of life and longed to see his gentle queen, Abol-rani, and his friend Bhatti. So off he flew to Ujjayini. By evening he was back in his own body, sitting on the verandah of his palace, drinking cool mango juice and recounting his adventures to his wife and Bhatti. Both of them, who loved him more than anyone in the world, were awestruck by the dangers he had undergone. 'All that is over,' said Vikram, King of Ujjayini. 'I am giving up my travels and will devote myself to governing my realm.'

'That is good news,' said Queen Abol-rani, smiling, and she kissed him gently.

Jagannath, the wandering story-teller, came to the end of his tale. The villagers went home and Jagannath headed for the wayfarers' shelter where he was to spend the night.

Some people from the north, who had come to visit the famous temple of Jnaneshvar in Alandi and had listened to the story of King Vikram, were also staying at the shelter. Next morning they offered to take Jagannath with them in their buffalo cart. They took him to the main road leading to the town of Nasik. There they said goodbye and Jagannath turned to a road which led to Dehu.

Before sunset Jagannath came to a village, where he was greeted and welcomed by old friends. He took his place in the tea-house on the village green and had a light meal. It wasn't long before a story-loving audience had gathered around him, and Jagannath began his tale.

How Krishna Lived Among the Shepherds and Destroyed the Demons

In far-off days a cruel king ruled over Braj, that pleasant country of hills, forests, copses and green pastures on the banks of the dark river, Yamuna.

It was a beautiful country. The fields yielded enough rice for everyone. The trees bore many fruits, large herds of cattle grazed on the pastures and the rivers, brooks and lakes were swarming with fish. The capital city of Mathura was imposing and wealthy. Proud peacocks strutted in its gardens and the many pools flowered with an abundance of white, blue and pink water-lilies. The streets were wide and lined with stores and shops, and the market place and town square were spacious. The temples of Mathura were so tall they could speak with the heavens; their brightly coloured colonnades, statues and splendid towers charmed the eye. From within came the majestic sounds of hymns and the intoxicating scent of incense.

And yet the people of Braj did not lead a happy life, for upon the throne of Mathura sat Kansa, an evil and cruel king, dreaded by all. Even his own father was powerless against his tyranny. By being cruel and malicious the king tried to cover up fear of his enemies. He trusted no one, not even his relatives and courtiers. And because he was unusually suspicious of plots against him, anyone who dared to look at him for more than a second was condemned immediately to death.

Kansa's uncle had a charming daughter called Devaki, a sweet maiden with long black hair, eyes as deep as pools in a valley and a voice as mellow as the call of the cuckoo in springtime. When she grew up it was time to find a suitable husband for her. Devaki's father, always mindful of Kansa's counsel, in order not to displease the king, visited him and asked for advice on the matter. Kansa suggested Vasudeva, a noble youth and gentleman, who was liked and esteemed by all good people.

Devaki's father consulted the astrologers and when the most appropriate and auspicious time had arrived he sent Vasudeva's father a message signifying that he would like to have Devaki marry his son. This was accepted with great pleasure and a few days later an impressive wedding procession set out for Mathura. At the head were father and son, followed by men-at-arms, groups of priests and holy men, and buffalo carts heavy with presents for the bride and her father.

Then in Mathura a magnificent wedding ceremony and a sumptuous feast took place, the splendour of which even a thousand poets would find it difficult to describe. King Kansa gave the happy couple fifteen thousand horses, four thousand elephants, eighteen hundred chariots, many slaves — men and women — fine fabrics and precious gowns, golden vessels and innumerable jewels and gems as a wedding present.

But suddenly thunder shook the heavens and a frightful voice sounded from above: 'Kansa, Kansa! The eighth child of Devaki and Vasudeva will be a son and he will be your undoing. He will kill you, because you are cruel and evil and will thus bring your unjust rule to an end!'

Startled, everyone stood frozen to the ground. Kansa shuddered in horror and in a fit of fury he pounced on the pale Devaki, caught her by the hair and dragged her to the ground, crying: 'When you tear a tree from the soil with the roots, how can it bear fruit? Hah! I shall kill you and then I shall rule without fear.'

Vasudeva was alarmed, but knew well from ancient books that evil cannot be fought by evil, only by goodness. He clasped his hands and said: 'Hear me, oh king of kings! No man in this land is as strong as you. We all live in the shadow of your gracious kindness. You are threatening a feeble woman with your sword, and your own cousin too. You will be mocked by everyone! Take my advice and let her go.'

Kansa hesitated, but still looked menacing, grinding his teeth. Vasudeva saw that first he must save Devaki and later on he would see if anything further could be done, for what the heavenly voice had ordained was irreversible and must come true. To Kansa he added: 'Let her go and I give you my word of honour that I shall surrender to you every son that she bears, to make sure you are safe.' Kansa accepted this, released poor Devaki and grunted: 'It is well, Vasudeva, that you have prevented me from committing a deadly sin. But do not forget your promise!'

The wedding guests then took their leave and gloomily went on their way.

As time passed Kansa killed all the children born to Vasudeva and Devaki. He had thus killed six sons of Vasudeva. The kind god Vishnu, who had seen all Kansa's depravities, decided to save Vasudeva's seventh son. From the gleam in his eye he created an ethereal vision in the shape of the woman Maya and said: 'Maya, fly to Mathura, where the cruel king Kansa is oppressing and murdering the people who worship me. Take the fruit of Devaki's womb and plant it into the womb of Rohini, who dwells in Nanda's house in Gokula.' Maya flew away and did what she had been told. Later Rohini gave birth to a boy called Balarama, of whom more shall be said in due time.

Kansa was informed of this by his demons, but it did not bother him since he only feared the eighth son, Krishna. He summoned Vasudeva to come and said sternly: 'You must do exactly what I ask! You must surrender me your eighth son, and I will grant you any wish that will not interfere with my plans.' He ordered the guards to put Vasudeva and Devaki in chains and throw them into a small dark room. All around he placed demons and evil spirits armed to the teeth, and then he went to the temple, where he prayed fervently that everything should turn out well for him. The foolish man completely forgot that what had been ordained by the heavenly voice could never be revoked. The next morning he ordered his strongest warriors to surround the room with elephants, lions and wild dogs. His intention was to kill the child as soon as it was born and thus be rid of the terrible fear that wrung his heart.

It was at midnight on a Wednesday in the eighth month of the dark half of the Month of the Rains that Krishna was born in all his sublime beauty. He was as dark as a cloud heavy with rain, his face was as bright as the full moon and his eyes were like water-lilies. He was wrapped in a yellow gown, adorned with a gorgeous diadem and wore a garland around his neck. In his four hands he held the symbols of his divine power: the shell, the discus, the club and the water-lily.

An unusual, joyous feeling spread throughout the country. The trees blossomed and bore delicious fruit. Lakes, pools, rivers and brooks filled with sweet sparkling water. Gods and demi-gods in their flying chariots soared above the whole country of Braj, and heavenly nymphs danced to the music of divine musicians. Flowers and drops of sweet scent showered from the skies. Vasudeva and Devaki were stunned by Krishna's resplendent appearance. They clasped their hands and bowed to him, their hearts cold with fear of the malevolent Kansa and his guards. But Krishna said in a sweet voice: 'Fear not, for I have come upon this earth to save you all, and justly to punish the wicked. But the time is not yet ripe, and I must hasten to Gokula to shepherd Nanda and his wife Yashoda. Take me there, Vasudeva.' And he turned into a crying baby. Devaki gently took him in her arms and gave him her breast. Krishna drank eagerly.

'You must save him from Kansa,' said Devaki to her husband. 'He wants to kill him,' replied Vasudeva helplessly. 'We are bound in heavy chains and, what is more, surrounded by three rows of guards and wild beasts!' But hardly had he uttered those words, when their fetters fell off by themselves, the prison door unlocked itself and all the guards and beasts fell fast asleep. Vasudeva put Krishna in a basket and, carrying him on his head, hastened to Gokula. When he arrived at the river Yamuna a tiger roared close behind him. 'This is the end,' he thought. 'A deep river in front of me and no boat, and a tiger at my back!' Nevertheless he stepped into the water and waded towards the opposite bank. The water became deeper and deeper but when it reached up to Vasudeva's mouth, Krishna put his leg forth from the basket, touched the surface and the water fell away. Vasudeva then had no trouble in crossing the river.

The night before, a daughter had been born to Nanda and his wife Yashoda, and when Vasudeva arrived all three of them were asleep. Vasudeva quietly took the baby girl, laid down Krishna in place of her in the crib, and returned to Mathura.

Devaki was happy that little Krishna was safe and said: 'What matter if Kansa kills us now that Krishna is saved!' The chamber door locked itself again, the fetters closed around Vasudeva's limbs and the guards and beasts woke up. The baby girl cried. The guards, who were watching near the chamber, heard her and took up their arms. The elephants trumpeted, the lions roared and the dogs howled. One of the guards ran to King Kansa, rushed into his chamber unannounced, and exclaimed: 'Oh King of Kings! Your enemy has come upon this earth.'

The king swooned in horror.

When he regained consciousness he roared like a wounded beast of prey and, with his hair dishevelled and perspiring in mortal fear, he grasped his sword and dashed out of his chamber. All out of breath he came to Devaki and grabbed the child from her hands. Poor Devaki, her hands clasped, cried: 'Do not kill the baby, cousin. After all, it is not a boy! You have already killed so many of my children. At least spare her! Do not add to your crimes!'

Kansa turned purple and with bloodshot eyes gasped: 'You shall never have her alive! It has been ordained that your eighth child will be my undoing, and though it be a girl that could come true. But I shall prevent it from happening!' He rushed to the courtyard and was about to dash the baby against the stone pavement. But just then the gods intervened, took the child away from him and raised it to the heavens. From the heights above, the little girl called to Kansa: 'A curse upon

you! Your despatcher has already been born and you are forfeit to death! Nothing can save you now!'

All of a sudden Kansa seemed to have lost his arrogance. He went back to Devaki and Vasudeva, with his own hands took off their fetters and started lamenting: 'Woe is me, what a terrible sin I have committed! How can I ever atone for all my crimes? What stands written in the book of Fate cannot be changed, but how is it that a girl was born to you when it should have been Krishna? I do not understand this.' He took both of them to his palace, clothed them with precious gowns and served them select food and beverages. For the time being his pride was gone.

When the shepherd Nanda and his wife Yashoda woke up in Gokula they noticed that in place of the baby girl Krishna lay in the crib. They were very happy and saw that what the kind god Vishnu had once promised them in a dream had really come true. Nanda at once called the astrologers and let them read the stars. They said: 'According to the stars and our books, this boy was born in a blessed year, a favourable month, a happy day and a lucky hour. He is God incarnate and will kill all the demons and evil spirits in order to rid the world of their cruel rule. He shall be called the Lord of the shepherds and will protect the country of Braj, and all the righteous will sing his praises.'

Nanda, pleased with the prophecy, rewarded the astrologers with two hundred thousand white cows, adorned with golden chains, silver-shoed and blanketed in silk. Now the musicians began to play, the dancers began to dance and the singers began to sing. All the shepherds of Gokula came with their families. Everyone rejoiced and congratulated Nanda and Yashoda. Then they feasted, drinking, eating and chewing betel rolls. This went on for several days.

However, the evil King Kansa sent forth one demon after another to search for Krishna and to kill him immediately. Knowing this, Nanda felt great anxiety.

It did not take long for Kansa to find out Krishna's whereabouts. At once he summoned the changeable demoness Putana and said to her: 'Putana, go to Gokula and kill the child born to Yashoda and Nanda, for he is my enemy!' Putana, her evil soul rejoicing, changed into a beautiful lady attired in a gorgeous gown and adorned with precious jewels. Looking exactly like the goddess Lakshmi, Vishnu's wife, she conjured up a deadly poison in her bosom and set out for Gokula. There she entered Nanda's house, asking for refreshment. Everyone liked her and soon Yashoda and she became friends. The cunning Putana feigned great admiration for Krishna as he lay in the cradle. She stroked and fondled him and eventually took him in her arms, to feed him. No one restrained her as she seemed so kind and charming! Little Krishna grasped her poisonous breast with both his hands and sucked, and sucked and sucked, until he sucked all the life out of the demoness. Putana cried out in deadly anguish, but to no avail. Her beauty began to vanish and she became a hideous demoness again. All were surprised at the ugliness of the corpse and Nanda said: 'This must have been some beastly demoness. It is well that Krishna has deprived her of life.'

Wicked Kansa kept on sending demons and evil spirits against Krishna, but all in vain. Krishna was twenty-seven days old when he killed the next demon, and another one paid with his life for threatening Krishna when he was five months old. It appeared as though little Krishna benefited from all of Kansa's intrigues; he grew unbelievably fast and was a very lively child. Months and years passed, and all the time Kansa never gave up trying to destroy Krishna. His efforts met with no success, and this made him all the more furious.

Once, on the occasion of Krishna's birthday, when Nanda had invited all his relatives and friends to the celebration, the subject of Kansa's persistent attacks was brought up. Then Nanda spoke thus: 'Kansa is a powerful king and his anger is boundless. His demons are incessantly crawling, climbing and flying to our Gokula, disturbing our peaceful lives. We are not safe enough here. Perhaps we should move to some other place, where there would be enough water and pasture for our cattle and where we could lead a happier life.' Nanda's brother Upananda suggested: 'Let's settle in Brindavana, the forest of the goddess Brinda, the Basil. We are sure to like it there and to get on well, because it is a peaceful and pleasant place, rich in all that shepherds and their flocks need.'

Everybody agreed with this. When they had eaten and drunk well Nanda asked the astrologer which would be the most opportune time to move from Gokula to Brindavana. The astrologer studied the position of the celestial bodies, consulted his book and finally said that the most opportune time would be the next morning at sunrise, for so said the

Tales Told by the Wanderer in Dehu

stars, planets and constellations; and moreover the moon, the nearest of the heavenly bodies, would be standing straight ahead of them in the direction of their journey, which was the most opportune of all signs. After this prophecy all the shepherds and shepherdesses went home to prepare for the journey. They put all their belongings on heavy two-wheeled carts drawn by black buffaloes, and at first light they crossed the river Yamuna. By evening they had reached their destination. There they held a divine service in honour of the goddess Brinda and established a new community. They began to live happily in peace and prosperity.

Krishna was now five years old and was always pleading with Yashoda to let him go and graze the cows and calves with the other boys. But Yashoda was against this, saying: 'There are plenty of herdsmen and farm hands; what good would you be there? You would only come to harm. You are a naughty and mischievous boy. I want to keep my eyes on you to make sure you do not get into trouble!' But Krishna, a wilful boy, said sulkily: 'All right, if you do not let me go to pasture with the rest of the boys, I will not eat anything.' What could poor Yashoda do with him? With a heavy heart she let him go, saying to the herdsmen: 'Take Krishna and Balarama with you today but do not let them out of your sight. And come back before the evening!' She gave each of them a big lunch-packet and let them drive the cattle to the pastures. But she was very worried about them.

The boys took the cows and the calves to graze on the banks of the Yamuna river. The grass there was thick and succulent and so they let the cows take care of themselves, and played together merrily.

All of a sudden one of Kansa's demons, changed into a calf, came towards them. Krishna said to Balarama: 'Watch out, another of Kansa's demons is approaching!' The cows and the calves scattered and the herdsmen hid wherever they could. The demon pretended to be grazing, but when he came closer Krishna made a dash at him, and catching him by the hind leg flung him on the ground with such force that the demon was dead on the spot. News of this reached the wicked King Kansa in no time and he was furious. Immediately he sent another demon in the form of a heron which paced the river bank. The herdsmen said to Krishna: 'Little brother, that must be a demon again. Look at the nasty way he is peering at us. However are we going to escape him?'

'There is no need to fear,' answered Krishna, walking towards the heron. The great bird picked him up with its long beak and swallowed him. But Krishna grew extremely hot in its belly, burning the heron so fiercely that it had no choice but to spit him out. Krishna caught hold of its beak, stepped on its neck and tore off its head. The herdsmen were terrified at first and wondered what they would say to Yashoda. However, seeing it had all turned out well and that Krishna could handle any demon, they laughed and frolicked through the afternoon, returning home before evening in high spirits.

Another time King Kansa sent forth the younger brother of the demoness Putana, whom Krishna had killed shortly after he was born. This demon, in the form of a huge python, lay in wait in the forest. Its jaws were wide open and the herdsmen saw it from afar. 'What kind of a huge hill is that? And that enormous cave! They never used to be here,' they wondered, not realizing that it was a huge python. Inquisitively, they walked right up to the horrid jaws, considering whether they should dare to step inside. Suddenly the python took a deep breath and sucked all the herdsmen, Krishna, the cows and the calves into its mouth, a stinking, slimy place full of poisonous vapours. The herdsmen were terrified, and the cows and calves mooed in fear. But Krishna began to grow larger and larger until he was a thousand times bigger than before; the python burst, and that was the end of it.

So Krishna killed many demons and evil spirits, and wicked King Kansa sat on his throne gritting his teeth and cursing because all his schemes came to nothing. Of course, the boys told their parents all about Krishna's adventures and everybody marvelled at his feats and was even fonder of him than before.

And every year on the fourteenth day of the dark half of the Month of Chicks, all the people of Braj would put on their best clothes and decorate their cleanly swept yards with intricate designs sprinkled on the dark ground with rice flour, saffron and sandalwood powder; the women would bake all sorts of cakes and pastries; and then all would assemble and in the smoke of incense and the light of oil lamps perform a ritual in honour of the god Indra. This had been done since time immemorial, for Indra was the highest of all gods, and he was their king.

That year too they were preparing for a big celebration. Krishna came to Yashoda and asked her: 'What are you preparing for? Is there a holiday coming?' Yashoda, who had her hands full of work, answered curtly: 'Look, my boy, I don't know whether I'm standing on my head or my feet; go and ask your father.' So Krishna went and asked Nanda: 'What kind of a celebration is there going to be? Which of the gods are we going to worship? What salvation does he bring to people, what gifts does he bestow on them, what good does he do them? Please explain it to me!'

Nanda answered kindly: 'Don't you know that it is the god Indra, lord of the clouds and rain, king of the gods, who awaits our offerings? It is by his grace that the world fares well, that the grass and the corn grow, that the trees, shrubs and herbs blossom, and it is thanks to him only that all creatures are provided with food. Since long ago our ancestors have all sacrificed to him, as we do now, and as our descendants will do in days to come.'

'But, Father,' objected Krishna, 'perhaps our ancestors did so because they did not know any better. They could not see what was really important and did not follow the right path. True, Indra did penance and tormented himself, proving the power of his mind, and the gods elected him their king. It is also true that he killed several evil spirits and demons and freed imprisoned streams to save all living creatures from death. But afterwards he hid like a jackal and has never done a good deed since. Why should we go on worshipping him? Everything that happens is ordained by fate, not by Indra's wishes. Only fate decides the lives of all of us, whether we be happy, rich, have brothers and sisters, wives, children, or cattle. If Indra really is the lord of the clouds and rain, why does he let the earth be burned by the scorching sun for eight long months? It is no thanks to Indra that afterwards everything is refreshed by the moisture of the rains, that the grass, herbs, shrubs, trees and all living creatures have food. Think of it, Father! We are shepherds, we live close to nature, in the forest among the hills and pastures — those are the lords we depend upon and should therefore worship. So from now on, we should not bring sacrifices to Indra, but to our hill, Govarddhana.'

Nanda was perplexed. He went to the village green where the shepherds sat and talked about many things, and repeated to them what Krishna had just told him. The shepherds thought the matter over and in the end decided that Krishna was right. 'Yes, of course,' they exclaimed, their voices mingling, 'that boy has more sense than all

of us!' And they decided that the next day they would not sacrifice to the god Indra but would go and worship the Govarddhana hill instead. And so they did.

Early at sunrise all the shepherds, the shepherdesses, and their children washed, put on their best clothes, took all the necessary things — bells, dulcimers, bowls, vessels, trays, jugs, cups, food-offerings, incense, lamps, corn and rice, sacrificial flowers and wreaths — and with music and songs the procession set out for the Govarddhana hill. On arriving there, they laid everything they had brought on the hill, and so the whole of Govarddhana was soon covered with sugar tarts, syrup, crunch, honey, chips, dough-nuts, coconut balls, meringues, frothed cakes, fritters, cream-pretzels, fruit rusks, almond biscuits, butter crisps, salt crackers, spiced rolls, sprinkled cakes and sweet-meats of all kinds. Besides these, there were other offerings: rice, corn, sesame, fruit, flowers and the coloured kumkum powder. All around the oil-lamps twinkled brightly, and the air was full of the sweet smell of incense-smoke. They decorated the peak of the hill with a beautiful wreath, made from the loveliest flowers, and around it they strewed betel leaves, almonds, pistachios and sultanas. Then the sacrificial priest performed the ceremony of worship as prescribed by ancient custom.

All the shepherds and shepherdesses had enjoyed this very much, and now Krishna decided to play another of his tricks. He created a second imposing body for himself and, dressed in a distinguished-looking gown, adorned and impressive, he appeared from the mountain to the rejoicing people of Brindavana. Standing among them in his first body he shouted: 'Behold the mighty Govarddhana, lord of the hills, mounds, and hillocks, who has appeared to us to show that he appreciates our pure hearts and sincere minds!'

The shepherds said to one another: 'You see, it's true. Indra never came to us, but this one we can all see, and we like him very much.' And they handed him plates, bowls and trays loaded with delicious titbits. Govarddhana ate and ate until he had eaten up all the good things the shepherds and shepherdesses had offered him in such enormous quantities. They were all very happy that he had not left a single morsel, and they finished by walking clockwise around the hill in veneration, then returning to Brindavana. There they painted all the bulls, cows and calves in bright colours and adorned them with bells. It was a day of joy.

The king of gods, Indra, who had waited for the usual offerings in vain, was very displeased. He summoned all the gods to him and asked: 'Do you know to whom the people of Braj brought offerings yesterday?' The gods sadly bowed their heads and answered: 'Lord, everyone worships and reveres you except the people of Brindavana; they are not disloyal of their own accord, but they have been provoked against you by Nanda's son, Krishna. He was the one who persuaded them to sacrifice to the hill Govarddhana.'

Indra became angry and said in a stern voice that resounded throughout the heavens: 'They are living well, their herds are multiplying, they are prospering, and their children are growing up healthy. Therefore they have become proud and have rejected the old customs. But they had better not trifle with me; I shall punish and humble them as they deserve.' He turned to the commander-in-chief of his cloud--army and ordered him: 'Take all your detachments, squads and units and pour down the greatest torrent of rain over all Braj, but most of all over the village Brindavana and the hill Govarddhana. Wash away every one of the arrogant shepherds with their herds so that no trace of them is left.'

The commander-in-chief bowed respectfully, lifted clasped hands to his brow and backed out of the throne-room of the king of gods, Indra. Immediately, the cloud-army charged through the skies. All the clouds — the white, the misty and the black — soaked up as much water as they could carry, surrounded Braj and poured down terrible torrents of rain, flooding the country. The shepherds were startled and in their fright they ran to Nanda's house, calling to Krishna: 'This must be Indra's punishment! It has never rained as much as this! Help us now, Krishna, you must help us, or we shall all perish with our cattle. This will be the end of us! It is a visitation from Indra!'

Krishna calmly said: 'Shake off your anxiety and forget your fears. Come with your children and your cattle to the Govarddhana hill.' Before the shepherds arrived there, he heated up the hill, by power of concentration, until it was like a glowing piece of coal, then he tore it off the ground and placed it on the protruding stone of the ring he wore on the middle finger of his left hand. And all the shepherds with their children and cattle took shelter under the hill so that the torrent of rain, violent and destructive though it was, could not harm them. They never stopped wondering at what Krishna could accomplish. 'Friends, it is really a miracle,' they said to one another. 'Krishna cannot be an ordinary man; perhaps he is our forefather, who has been born among us again. He may be the god of gods himself. Could an ordinary mortal carry a whole mountain on his finger?'

Indra's cloud-army poured down rain incessantly, but not a drop fell on the people of Brindavana. The king of gods, Indra, raved with fury and abused the commander-in-chief, but things were as they were and nothing could be done about it. The terrible torrent lasted seven days and seven nights until at last the clouds — the white, the misty and the black — clasped their hands, bowed their heads and said to Indra: 'We have come to an end, oh Lord. We have poured down all the water we had; there is none left to rain with. It is all drained away and we cannot wring out a single tear more.' At this, Indra, though he was discontent and angry, began to wonder: 'Who can have the power and strength to resist my anger and to hold up a hill as large as Govarddhana above the people of Brindavana? It is very strange indeed.' He did not know what to think of it, and so he went home, followed by the bedraggled clouds. The sky cleared, the sun began to shine and the shepherds saw that they had been saved. Krishna put the hill back in its place and they all went home.

The shepherds and the shepherdesses admired Krishna's strength and cleverness. They fawned on him, flattered him and embraced him,

Tales Told by the Wanderer in Dehu

especially the shepherdesses, who could not take their eyes off his handsome figure. And in the evening, when they were boisterously celebrating Krishna's victory over Indra, they all wanted to dance only with Krishna. The flutes, oboes, drums and the dulcimers played merry dance-tunes, and the eager shepherdesses could not wait for Krishna to invite them to dance. In order to satisfy all the young ladies without keeping them waiting, Krishna used a spell to make several apparitions look exactly like himself, and these danced with the eager shepherdesses while Krishna was able to dance the whole evening with his beloved Radha.

The next day they went to pasture as usual. Krishna played the flute, Balarama and the other shepherds sang, the cows and the calves mooed, the birds twittered and above them shone the bright sun. On that day Indra, seated on his elephant, came out of the divine world, followed by a host of gods. Realizing that it was futile to try to overcome Krishna, he came to pay him homage. He was some distance away when he saw Krishna among the shepherds and the cattle, and he dismounted from the elephant and approached him barefoot. Trembling, he fell in tears at Krishna's feet: 'Lord of the whole country of Braj, have mercy on me and forgive me for being so bold as not to believe in your greatness. I was governed by pride and blinded by arrogance. Forgive me for wanting to do harm to you and the people of Braj.' When Krishna saw him so sad and genuinely humble he took pity upon him and said kindly: 'Rise, Indra, I forgive and pardon you. You can see for yourself that pride and arrogance do harm only to their bearer. Never again be proud or arrogant, for pride drives away reason, and arrogance suppresses prudence. Anyone so foolish becomes the laughing stock of all.' Indra was very happy that Krishna had forgiven him and, bowing gratefully, he returned to the heavens, followed by his retinue.

One day old Akrura, Krishna's uncle from Mathura, came to Brindavana. He bowed to Krishna and Krishna bowed to him, and then the uncle saluted Nanda, Yashoda and all his relatives. He told them that Kansa's cruelty was boundless, that things were worse than ever in Mathura, that no one could be sure of his life, for Kansa in his fits of rage gave the most terrible orders to his guards and myrmidons. 'Our beautiful capital city of Mathura,' said Akrura, 'is suffering under the despotism of a spiteful murderer. Whatever are we going to do?'

Krishna was among those listening to his uncle's account, and afterwards he said: 'The time has come for me to put an end to Kansa's crimes. Tomorrow I shall go with you to Mathura, Uncle.'

The following day a group of shepherds went with Akrura; besides Krishna and Balarama, Nanda, his brother Upananda and several others set out for Mathura. They set up tents outside the walls of Mathura, and Krishna with Balarama went to take a look at Kansa's residence. As they were passing through the town people pointed at them in admiration, saying: 'That is Krishna from Brindavana, the one who has killed so many of Kansa's evil spirits! And his brother Balarama is with him. You see, they come right here, fearing nothing!' The citizens of Mathura threw flowers over the brothers, and showered them with scents and sandalwood powder. They were happy that Krishna had come and guessed that Kansa's cruel reign would not last much longer. And any of the citizens who had caught a glimpse of Krishna took a strong liking to him.

The gate of Kansa's palace was guarded by several rough-looking soldiers. When Krishna and Balarama approached, their lieutenant shouted: 'Get away, you riff-raff! This is the gate to the king's palace! This is no place for you!' Krishna and Balarama took no notice of him and got into the palace. They hurried to the armoury, where the enormous bow of the terrible god Shiva had been placed. Krishna took it, bent it — and the enormous bow cracked like a sugar-cane stalk. At the same moment Kansa's guards pounced upon the two brothers. But they were powerless against Krishna and Balarama.

Meanwhile, King Kansa was sitting in the chamber of his favourite wives. When he heard the sound of the cracking of Shiva's bow, he cowered in fear. He was horror-struck, but his bloodthirstiness showed itself once more. He mercilessly knocked down the courtier who brought him news of Krishna's arrival and then stabbed him to the heart. 'To arms, everyone!' he howled. 'Fight those shepherds! Kill them! Murder them! By strength or by trickery, it does not matter how!'

All who could carry arms immediately attacked Krishna and Balarama. It seemed as if huge swarms of bees were assaulting a single flower. The battle was savage. Krishna said to Balarama: 'Brother, we ought to be getting back, or Nanda will be worried that we are away so long. Let's hurry up. Beat those henchmen down by twos or threes and get it over and done with.' They did away with the armed men in no time, and then calmly returned to the shepherds' tents outside the city.

Kansa was horrified. He went to the temple but could not concentrate on his prayers. So he went to bed, but could not fall asleep and tossed about until daybreak. Then at last he fell asleep and dreamt that he was standing in the cemetery, his body bleeding, bloodstained flowers around his neck, foul blood splashed all around, and the spirits of the dead dancing and howling and playing with their skulls as if they were balls. Their dry bones creaked to the rhythm of the dance. He woke up almost dead with fright, but his cruelty and bloodthirstiness did not forsake him. The greater his fear, the more evil he became. He summoned his counsellors, creatures as bad as he was, and ordered them: 'Have the jousting grounds set up and decorated. Then invite all the courtiers, the gentry, the burghers, the merchants and the tradesmen, and above all those shepherds from Brindavana. Use force to bring anyone who refuses to come. I shall challenge Krishna to a contest!' But he did not mention that he was contemplating trickery and that his heart was cold with fright.

Soon the jousting grounds were set up, the seats covered with velvet, the flags and the banners flying, and the musicians playing. The first of the guests began to arrive. The gods, their curiosity aroused, came to watch the contest, floating through the heavens on their flying chariots. King Kansa did not arrive until all places were full up to the very last. Then he took his seat on the grandstand, beneath a splendid canopy, and pretended to be carefree, though in his heart of hearts he had a feeling of foreboding.

Krishna and Balarama were a little late. When they arrived at the gate of the jousting grounds they saw an enormous elephant, strong as a thousand ordinary elephants, standing in their way to the entrance. The perfidious Kansa had it placed there on purpose, hoping it would kill both brothers before they entered the grounds. It blocked the gate completely, leaving not even a tiny chink. Krishna said to the herdsman: 'Step aside a bit with the elephant. We have been invited here. Can't you see we cannot get inside?' The herdsman retorted rudely: 'Push it away yourselves!' And he pricked the elephant with a goad to enrage it. The elephant pounced on Balarama, but he gave it such a blow with his fist, that it backed away, curled up its trunk and roared in pain. The herdsman, who was aware that if he allowed the brothers to enter the grounds he would be cruelly put to death by Kansa, goaded the elephant all the more. The animal caught Krishna with its trunk, intending to dash him to the ground, but Krishna at once made himself tiny and slipped from the elephant's grip, safe and sound. Then the brothers, standing one in front and the other behind the huge elephant, took it by trunk and tail and after first swinging it, threw it high up in the air. The elephant fell to the ground and never got up again. Krishna went to it and gave it a last blow on the temple. The elephant's tail jerked and a river of black blood gushed out of its muzzle. It was dead.

Krishna tore out its tusks, gave one to Balarama and kept the other one himself. And so they walked into the jousting grounds, greeted by the rejoicing shepherds and burghers, while Kansa and his guards and demons sat in gloomy silence.

The terrified king suddenly shouted, his voice faltering in anger and fear: 'Beat them and kill them!' All of Kansa's fighters surrounded Krishna and Balarama. One of them, Chanura, stepped forward and said provokingly: 'Our king is sadly troubled today. We must cheer him up a bit. Come on, Krishna, if you are not afraid!' And he grabbed Krishna. Their arms gripped, their heads clashed, their legs entwined and they stared at each other menacingly.

'This is not a fair fight,' said the Mathurans to each other. 'The king is treacherous and mean. Chanura is a strong and experienced fighter, whereas Krishna is so young that Chanura can do what he likes with him.' But Krishna grasped Chanura and gave him a crushing embrace. Chanura grew limp and grunted, and his eyes bulged. When Krishna loosened his hold of him, Chanura fell to the ground dead.

Now all of Kansa's fighters fell upon the two brothers and a terrible battle ensued. Krishna and Balarama, endowed with godly strength, killed one fighter after another and threw their corpses aside on a heap. And the heap grew larger and larger. The Mathurans and the shepherds shouted with joy, the gods on their flying chariots laughed, the heavenly musicians played and the fairies danced. Kansa was pale as death. 'All men-at-arms, fall upon them!' he shouted, choking with rage. 'Kill Vasudeva and Devaki before their eyes, and also the shepherds. Then kill both the brothers!'

But it was of no avail. Krishna and Balarama took the tusks of the elephant which had had the strength of a thousand elephants and using them as a cudgel and a spear, they killed all of Kansa's men-at-arms. A tense silence fell over the jousting grounds.

Krishna started, and with a single flying jump landed on the grandstand where, beneath the silk canopy and wearing a gown of purple and gold, sat the once-so-proud King Kansa. He held a double-edged sword in his hand, his head was covered by a strong helmet. But his former pride and arrogance had melted away. He quivered and trembled, and his face was distorted with horror, anger and shame. He would have liked to run away and save at least his life, but he was ashamed to admit his cowardice. He swung his sword at Krishna furiously, but Krishna knocked off his helmet, caught him by the hair and threw him down from the grandstand. Kansa, whose bones had been broken by the fall, lay on the sand groaning. His eyes bulged with horror. Krishna called out from the grandstand: 'Hah, you evil king, you tyrant! This is the end of you. You will never again commit a crime, you villain!'

And he jumped down on top of the writhing Kansa. And so the worst king that ever ruled the country of Braj met his end.

All the villagers, children and grown-ups, listened in silence. The wandering story-teller picked up his iktar and played a little tune. Then he sang:

> 'Though the story seems a lie
> Truth is hidden from the eye.
> What's a lie and what is true?
> Make a guess, it's up to you.'

And he began another story.

The Doe-princess

Once upon a time there was a king whose favourite pastime was hunting. Almost every day, after he had carried out his royal duties, he would mount his horse and with a small number of courtiers, would ride into the forest. Often it happened that they were overtaken by night there, in which case they would spread their cloaks on the green grass and lie down to sleep, returning to the city in the morning.

The king had a favourite place deep in the forest, where the grass was particularly green, lush, thick and silky, and there he slept far better than on his royal bed. It was an extraordinary place, quite different from the other glades. The dense bushes surrounding it formed a natural arbour, which provided good shelter when the weather was bad.

Now it came to pass one day that a doe came to graze in this royal glade. The grass was so delicious that the doe came day after day, until there was nothing left to graze on. The king, who sometimes spent the night there, was surprised to see the grass all eaten, but he never set his eyes on the doe. The doe saw him often and found him very handsome.

After a time the doe gave birth to a son. The mother took good care of the baby and all the other animals helped as much as they could, and so the boy grew and prospered. When he reached the age of twelve he asked his mother-doe: 'Who is my father, Mother? Where is he?' The doe answered truthfully: 'Son, your father is the king. He lives with his queen and children in his palace in the capital city, and rules the whole of our country.'

'Allow me then to go to the capital city,' said the boy, 'I want to serve the king.' The mother-doe gave him permission. The boy said goodbye to his mother and went.

At the palace gate he told the guards that he had come to serve the king. The guards let him in not only because of what he told them, but because he so strongly resembled the king.

When the boy entered the throne-room and reverently bowed to the king, a deep silence followed. The king, his counsellors, and all the courtiers looked at the boy in amazement, not knowing what to think of it all. The king, who was the first to regain his composure, said: 'Who are you, child, and what brings you here?'

'My name is Hiran and my home is very far from here,' answered the boy. 'I have come to serve you, Your Majesty.'

The king asked: 'What kind of work would you like to do for me? You are still a very little boy.'

'I will do any work you require, sir,' said Hiran.

The king pondered a while and then he said: 'For the time being go to the kitchen and tell the chief cook it is my wish that he should treat you to the best dishes and drinks, as befits a guest from afar. Then come back and I shall give you work.' Hiran bowed and went.

The counsellors and the courtiers were about to leave too, but the king detained them: 'Stay awhile, I want to ask you something.' He turned to his oldest counsellor and said: 'Since you are experienced and wise, I ask you first, who does the boy who wants to serve me look like?'

The counsellor was very embarrassed and hesitated to reply: 'Your gracious Majesty, how can I say? I am old and my sight is not as good as it used to be. I cannot give an answer.'

'True, you are old, counsellor, but your sight is still good,' said the king, smiling. 'Speak up and say whom the boy resembles!'

'I may be mistaken,' the counsellor said reluctantly, 'but it seems to me that the boy resembles someone I know very well.'

'Who is it, then?' persisted the king. 'I order you to speak up!'

'But will you forgive me, my sovereign, if I am mistaken?' demanded the counsellor.

'That I promise you.'

And the counsellor said in a low voice: 'The boy resembles you strongly, sir. He looks more like you than any of your sons do.'

'Well,' remarked the king, 'your sight is not nearly as bad as you complained it is.' And then he asked the opinion of the rest of the counsellors and courtiers. They all confirmed that Hiran resembled the king more than any of the royal princes did.

The king decided to bring up Hiran with the princes. When Hiran returned to the throne-room, the king said to him: 'I shall employ you, Hiran. Your task will be to join the princes in all their games and studies.' Hiran bowed, and one of the courtiers led him to the princes.

Time passed and Hiran became more skilful at games and a better student than any of the princes were. The king liked him and was kind to him, but the queen secretly despised him and decided to get rid of him somehow.

One day, as Hiran was playing ball with the princes, the queen passed by and, by accident, the ball struck her on the head. It was not a hard blow but the queen began to cry and make a fuss, and went to her chamber, where she lay on the bed pretending to be seriously ill and dying.

When the king learned that the queen was ill he hurried to her and asked: 'What has happened? What's the matter? I shall call the doctor!'

The queen just sighed and groaned: 'Nothing can save me now! I am dying! That boy you are bringing up with our princes hit me on the head with a ball. He must have done it deliberately!'

The king looked at the queen and said: 'There are no marks on your head. Surely it cannot be so painful!'

'But it is painful!' cried the queen in tears. 'There is a terrible pain in my head. You can't see it.'

'Perhaps it really does hurt,' thought the king and tried to console her: 'Hush now, stop crying, it will only make you feel worse. I shall do anything you wish, but just stop crying.'

'Will you really do anything I wish?' asked the queen.

'Yes,' nodded the king.

'Then hang that boy who hit me!' exclaimed the queen vindictively. 'Hang him on the gallows! I will have no peace until he is hanged! Only then shall I get well again!'

But the king did not want to deprive Hiran of his life. So he summoned the hangman and ordered him to hang Hiran but to use the softest of ropes and to arrange things so that Hiran should stay alive, and that the rope should neither squeeze nor scratch his neck. The hangman carried out this order meticulously. The king placed a guard near the gallows to make sure no ill would befall Hiran, and returned to the palace.

Just then, in the forest, Hiran's mother-doe felt a strange restlessness in her heart. A feeling of foreboding, anxiety and fear drove her to the city. She ran almost the whole day and by evening came to the gallows, where her son Hiran was hanging.

'Woe is me,' cried the mother-doe in despair. 'What have you done, my son, to be punished so by the king?' For she thought that Hiran was dead. But Hiran answered her: 'Don't cry, mother. I am safe and sound. It was my stepmother who made the king hang me.' The doe stood on her hind legs, took Hiran off the gallows, and fondled him. Then she ran away, and returned with all sorts of fruit, which she gave Hiran to eat. She spent the whole night with him, then at dawn she put him back on the gallows and ran away.

The guard, who had witnessed all this, immediately reported it to the king. Marvelling at what he heard, the king ordered him: 'Go back to the gallows, take Hiran down, bring him to the kitchen and let him eat and drink well. Then put him to bed and let him have a good rest. But be careful lest the queen should see you. Come for me in the evening, when you will hang Hiran on the gallows again and I shall watch what happens. I must find out who Hiran and the doe are, and why he said that it was his stepmother who made me hang him.'

The guard obeyed the king's orders. When evening came the king took Hiran by the hand and the three of them went towards the gallows. The king said to Hiran, 'My dear boy, do it once again for my sake. I promise that no ill shall befall you, since I feel an unusual affection for you. I shall protect you from the queen's wrath, for I am the king, and nothing can happen without my knowledge and consent. But I must find out what is going on here.'

'Yes, my lord and king,' said Hiran, 'I will do as you wish. But please do not do anything rash or violent.'

'You need not fear that,' the king assured him.

The guard carefully hung Hiran on the gallows and then he and the king hid in the bushes nearby. Soon after nightfall the mother-doe appeared and, standing on her hind legs, took Hiran off the gallows. She fondled and embraced him and then refreshed him with all sorts of fruit. The king, watching them from the bushes, listened to their conversation. And all the time he wondered why Hiran called the doe his mother, and why he claimed that it was his stepmother who had made the king hang him, when it was the queen who had done this.

At daybreak the doe put Hiran back on the gallows and, bidding him farewell, said: 'This evening I will come again and will spend the whole night with you. I would like you to return to the forest with me, my son.' Suddenly the king sprang from the bushes and caught the doe.

'Let me go, please!' cried the doe. But the king held her firmly and did not loosen his grip. 'I shall not let you go until I find out who you are and who Hiran is, the boy who looks so much like me,' exclaimed the king. 'I must know!'

'I will gladly tell you everything, Your Majesty,' answered the doe, 'but first you must do what I ask of you.'

'What shall I do?' demanded the king, setting the doe free.

The doe said: 'First take Hiran off the gallows.' When the king had done so he asked: 'What now?'

'Now draw your sword,' said the doe, 'and cut off my head!' The king hesitated but the doe encouraged him: 'Do not hesitate, Your Majesty, cut it off!'

The king swung his sword with all his strength. No sooner had the two-edged sword touched the doe's neck than she disappeared, and in her place stood a beautiful princess. Hiran and the king gazed at her in amazement.

The princess spoke: 'I am the daughter of the king of Bhojpur. A wicked witch turned me into a doe because I refused to marry her hideous son, the wizard, and she told me that only the father of my son could break the spell and save me by cutting off my head. This has happened today, for Hiran is our son, oh king!'

Hiran fell into her arms, and the king was speechless with surprise. The princess told them how, as the doe, she used to graze in the very glade the king had chosen to sleep in when he went hunting; how she had brought up Hiran and how later on he had decided to go and serve the king. At last the king knew why Hiran resembled him so. He put his arms round him and said: 'Both of you, come with me to the royal palace, and we shall live together now that we have met so happily.' And they all went to the royal palace.

The king drove the evil queen out of the country and named Hiran his heir, because he was the wisest and cleverest of all the princes. Then in all glory, at a magnificent wedding ceremony, the king married the princess of Bhojpur, and they all lived happily ever after.

When Jagannath had finished his tale everybody went home and the story-teller went to the wayfarers' shelter. After making some tea for himsef in a teapot in the yard, he lay down to sleep. In the morning he bought a bunch of bananas at the bazaar and set out for Koregaon. Once there, he headed straight for the house of his old friend, a member of the elders' council, whose name was the same as his — Jagannath. The house consisted of one room, unfurnished except for a single chest, a shrine in the corner with a picture of the kind god Vishnu, and a few flowers and sticks of incense. In another corner there were some brass pots, a stone mortar for corn and beans, a stone slab for preparing food, a stone rolling-pin, a large jug of water, and some tins of flour, rice, lentils and other foodstuffs. Near the wall there were mats with blankets folded on them. The floor was of trodden earth.

The two Jagannaths exchanged friendly greetings, and Jagannath's wife prepared a dinner in honour of the distinguished guest. After dinner, when word had got round Koregaon that the wandering story-teller had come, everybody gathered on the village green under the spreading mango tree, and Jagannath began his story.

How
the Brave Prithviraj
Defended his Kingdom and Married
Princess Sanyogita

The ruler of Delhi, King Anangpal of the house of Tomar, arranged a glorious celebration on the occasion of the wedding of his daughter Kamla and King Someshvar of the house of Chauhan. The sumptuous feast lasted several weeks. Anangpal gave his daughter a dowry of five hundred slave girls, one thousand villages with all the land and serfs, elephants, horses, camels and bulls, lovely carriages, gold, jewels and precious stones, and also a citadel on the frontier, enclosed by fortifications and a deep moat.

The celebration was over, the guests departed, and Someshvar, after bidding farewell to his father-in-law, set out with his wife for the royal seat of Ajmer. It was a long caravan that left Delhi, for Anangpal and Someshvar were the two most powerful kings of those times.

Someshvar Chauhan also governed some of the neighbouring kingdoms and levied taxes on them. He was a sturdy figure, with black

Tales Told by the Wanderer in Koregaon

whiskers, and he ranked among the highest nobles of Rajput. His marriage to Kamla, of the Tomar dynasty in Delhi, only confirmed his power.

A year later a son was born to the royal couple in Ajmer, and was named Prithviraj. The astrologers divined that he had come into the world at a fortunate time, when the planets and the constellations were in the most favourable positions. When a special messenger brought King Anangpal the news that he had a fine grandson, he received a rich reward. Then the king held a splendid banquet, at which he got as drunk as a lord, from joy.

The whole of Ajmer also celebrated the birth of Someshvar's first-born son. There was dancing and singing and feasting all over the place. The gods rode across the skies in their flying chariots, strewing flowers on the earth and showering it with sweet-smelling rain. Kamla's sister Sursundri, the wife of Vijaypal, king of Kannauj, sent her little nephew a beautifully embroidered layette made of the softest fabric, and an engraved gold cup. Prince Prithviraj truly was born under a lucky star, for he had all the thirty-two signs of beauty, charm and success. During the splendid festivities in Ajmer, Delhi and Kannauj, thousands of priests, holy men and penitents were entertained, and several hundred iron-tipped chests of gold were distributed among the poor.

In the family of a poor but wise and learned Brahman another boy was born on the same day as Prithviraj; he was given the name Chand. Later on Chand became Prithviraj's most faithful friend and counsellor. He stood by him all his life and never forsook him.

Little Prithviraj grew eight times as fast as any other boy. When he was precisely one year, one month, one fortnight, one day, one hour, and one minute old, a distinguished ceremony took place at which the royal priest put a necklace of lion's claws around his neck. Prithviraj was a charming little boy. He had already learned to speak and his voice was as sweet as a bird's song. He had black curly hair and when he laughed, his lustrous little white teeth illumined everything around him like the full moon.

When the time came for him to begin his studies, a wise teacher educated the prince in fourteen sciences, and showed him how to write with a reed on silk scarves. He also tutored him in seventy-two arts, crafts and skills, as well as eighty-four branches of learning. He taught him six important languages and acquainted him with six doctrines of philosophy.

Old Anangpal, ruler of Delhi, had two daughters, Kamla and Sursundri, but no son. This troubled him, for he did not know to whom he should leave his kingdom. He summoned an astrologer, a holy man familiar with all things of mystery, and said to him: 'You are a wise man and know how to read the stars just as you read books. Tell me what will happen in the future, for I have no heir and will not live to have a son. I fear that after my death there will be trouble and a fight for the throne, which might cause the kingdom to fall and be plundered by foreign invaders. What do the stars say?'

The astrologer studied the vault of heaven and its glimmering lights for a long while and then he said: 'Your Majesty, it is true, you will never have a son. But do not fear, your kingdom will not fall. I see a boy in the kingdom of Mevat, in the royal seat of Ajmer, in Someshvar's royal palace. He is an excellent swordsman, is versed in the sciences and has great knowledge. It is your grandson Prithviraj. You must call him to Delhi and make him your heir. My inner sight shows me that under Prithviraj's rule your kingdom will flourish and prosper; Prithviraj will mercilessly vanquish the aggressive Afghani Turushkas who are encroaching on us from the north-west, and will bring glory to your house and to the house of Chauhan.'

'Yes, that is what I'll do,' thought King Anangpal and, having richly rewarded the astrologer, he allowed him to leave.

Meanwhile young Prithviraj thrived and became a man. His fame and popularity grew like knowledge in a good student's head; like the waxing moon on an autumn night; like maiden's breasts; like a shrewd merchant's purse; like a wise hermit's perception; like heaps of corn in the loft at harvest time; like new fabrics on looms; like the mass of dead enemies who had attacked our country. He was now twenty-two, strong and courageous. He had no equal in battle. His chest was as solid as a mountain peak, and his arms were feared by the enemy as if they were the god Indra's thundering clubs. Once he had taken a stand nobody could budge him. And he was as fast as the wind, whether in pursuit of the fleeing enemy in battle, or when following his hounds in the hunt.

Chand, the son of the poor sage, who had been born on the same day and at the same hour as Prithviraj, had become the prince's inseparable companion long ago. They became friends when they were boys. It happened one day when Prithviraj was playing a war game with the courtiers' and burghers' sons in front of the palace gates. The prince led one army, Chand the other. The battle was just about to begin when Chand stepped forward, raised his right arm, and trying to make his childish little voice sound like roaring thunder, recited the following verse:

'Sword in hand, prepared to slay,
Valiant soldiers are we all.
Elephants trumpet, horses neigh,
Conches sound the battle call!'

After this the battle was launched. It is not known which of the armies won, but after a truce was made Prince Prithviraj came to Chand and asked him: 'What was the verse you started the battle with?'

'Oh, I just made that up,' answered Chand simply. 'You see, I am a poet.' Prithviraj took a great liking to Chand. They became friends for life, and never forsook each other in times good or bad.

Some years later Prithviraj, Chand, and a large retinue were setting out for a hunt. The prince ordered the servants to get ready horses, elephants, beaters, tame leopards, hounds and a lavish picnic, and they rode out of the city gates. They were armed with bows and arrows, spears and lances, and each of the hunters had a shield as protection in case he should be attacked by a beast of prey. The forest resounded with the barking of dogs, the neighing of horses, the trumpeting of elephants and the roaring of leopards.

Innumerable was the game shot, ensnared, hunted down by the hounds or killed by the leopards. Many a stag and hind was pierced by the spears and lances, and the hunters on their swift horses and their stately elephants scrambled up the hillside, for close to the top there was more game. The forest grew denser all the time, the lianas twined up the ancient furrowed tree-trunks, and the rich foliage cast a pleasant, cool shadow. The flowers were as numerous as the leaves, though brighter in colour and more varied in shape. But the hunters noticed none of this beauty; they pursued their prey, their weapons ready to deal blows of death.

Underneath a spreading mango tree deep in the forest a hermit, meagre in body and wise in mind, sat with crossed legs. His skin was weather-beaten as if he had been in a forest fire. All he possessed was a rudraksh beadroll, the leopard-skin he wore, a coconut shell for water, and a grass mat to sleep on which, when the rains came, he used as a protection against the downpour. He was a holy man to whom the mystery of life and death had been revealed and to whom nothing remained unknown. His deep dark eyes shone with the light of knowledge. Chand was the only one of the hunters who noticed him. The rest rushed by like a tempest. Chand realised at once that here was a rare and distinguished holy man. He longed to speak to him. Approaching him with his hands clasped at his brow, he said: 'I bow to you, oh being that hast no beginning and no end. It is the greatest honour of my life to be able to meet you and bow unto you.' He lowered his head to the ground and humbly touched the holy man's feet. 'Oh, saint! Surely the spirit of the creator Brahma, Vishnu's keeper and Shiva's destroyer, dwells in you. I bow to you, oh holy man! Look upon me kindly!'

The hermit said: 'Welcome, Chand. I knew you would come today. I have a gift for you, which will be of value also to Prince Prithviraj.' He paused for a while and then continued: 'I will tell you a magic formula. Whenever you pronounce it fifty-two miraculous warriors, endowed with mysterious power and superhuman strength, will appear before you, ready to carry out any command you may give.'

Chand could not believe his ears. 'Come closer, my son,' said the holy man, 'so that I may whisper the magic formula in your ear.' And he whispered: 'Om tat sat, om tam tham, dam dham nam, om hrim svaha!'

Chand learned the magic formula by heart, thanked the holy man, bowed to him and mounting his horse rode at full speed to catch up with the hunters. He galloped through the dense jungle where one could see no farther than two leaps of a horse. Meanwhile Prince Prithviraj with his courtiers continued on his white elephant, holding back the hunting leopards on silken leashes. The group was followed by two-wheeled carts, drawn by buffaloes, and servants who picked up the game that had been shot and loaded it onto the carts. Chand caught up with the hunters and immediately dashed after the fleeing game. As the hunting continued, the carts were so overloaded with deer and birds that they began to sink into the ground.

When they were all tired, the hunters came together to rest and to refresh themselves with a delicious meal and strong drinks. They sat down on embroidered blankets beneath gold-and-pearl-fringed canopies; the servants then served food and drink. Everyone had enjoyed the hunting and praised Prithviraj for enabling them to spend such a pleasant day and for treating them to such a feast. Then Chand, the poet, stood up and recited an ode in honour and praise of Prithviraj and all the guests who had participated in the hunting.

As they sat there feasting and chatting merrily, a hungry tiger prowled stealthily towards the tethered horses and elephants, ready to kill and devour one of them. The animals, sensing it from afar, neighed and trumpeted, but the gleeful hunters took no notice. When the tiger got closer, the elephants and horses tore away from their ropes and ran loose: the horses headed away from the tiger but the elephants charged, trying to gore it with their tusks and trample it to death. There was a great turmoil. Forgetting their drinks, the hunters sprang to their feet and tried to calm the frightened animals, but all in vain. They tumbled over one another with no result. Suddenly Chand remembered the magic formula and quickly pronounced it. In an instant fifty-two miraculous warriors appeared before him and in a single voice said: 'What are your orders, sir?'

'Help us!' cried Chand. 'A tiger has scared our horses and elephants and they have run away. Hurry up and catch them!'

The warriors bowed and got to work. Immediately all the horses and elephants were tied to their places, and the tiger, captured and bound, lay at Chand's feet. The miraculous warriors bowed again and vanished before he could thank them. The hunters looked on dumbfounded.

'Chand, dear Chand,' said Prince Prithviraj, 'what is this? I had no idea you could practise such magic. Tell us all about it!' And Chand described how he met the holy man and bowed to him, how he received a gift — the magic formula. The prince and the hunters would hardly have been able to believe it all, had not the tiger lain bound in front of Chand. It lay there seemingly calm, but there was a fierce gleam in its eyes, and the tip of its tail whisked angrily. 'And the proof that all I have said is the bare truth,' said Chand, turning to Prithviraj, 'is this tiger, who caused all the trouble. I give it to you as a token of my lasting esteem and respect.'

The chase was over and they all returned home, taking the game with them. Rumour has it that some of Prithviraj's guests afterwards tried very hard to find the holy man and to obtain the magic power he had bestowed on Chand, but they never found him. He had disappeared as if the earth had swallowed him up.

Just at that time the king of Delhi, Anangpal, sent a letter to Ajmer, to his son-in-law Someshvar, in which he told him that he had decided to hand over his kingdom to his son, Prithviraj, and invited them both to come to Delhi. The letter was delivered by a large group of courtiers from Delhi. All were attired in splendid gowns; their white blood horses were caparisoned in gold and scarlet and had beautifully ornamented saddles. King Someshvar summoned an assembly to which, besides Prithviraj, he invited the guests from Delhi and the nobility of the Ajmer court. And, of course, the prince's friend Chand was also invited.

When everyone was present Someshvar turned towards his son and said: 'Our house — and especially you, dear son — has been greatly honoured. King Anangpal Tomar, whom the gods have not blessed with a son and heir, has chosen you, Prince Prithviraj, to inherit his kingdom. He has invited us to come to Delhi without delay. Prepare the chariots, saddle the horses and elephants. We shall set out for the journey early in the morning.'

When they arrived in Delhi, Anangpal arranged for a feast in honour of the guests from Ajmer, and at a moment the astrologers considered propitious, he presented his grandson Prithviraj with the coronation deed, which he had written on silk in his own hand. Then he led him to the golden throne. The moment the prince sat on it everybody cheered him, and the drums sounded like a heavy thunderstorm in the rainy season. A hundred elephant-riders and a thousand horsemen rode through the city, throwing gold coins, pearls and precious stones to the people. And so Prithviraj became the ruler of Delhi.

In those days the ruler of Afghanistan was Sultan Shihabuddin Ghori, one of the greediest and most warlike of the Turushkas. Watching Prithviraj's kingdom of Delhi with greed and suspicion, he finally decided to attack it with his army. He first summoned the commanders and consulted them. Then he ordered the army to prepare: 'Tomorrow we march to Delhi!' The next day the Afghan army was quickly approaching the frontier of Prithviraj's country.

King Prithviraj happened to be hunting close to the border with some of his courtiers. When scouts brought him news of the Turushka campaign, he called a conference of war. Counsellor Kaimas gave orders to beat the war-drums and in no time the Rajput army was ready. Leading it was Prince Prithviraj, astride his splendid white stallion, at the head of innumerable soldiers. The scouts discovered that the Afghan assailants had pitched camp and were resting, for it had never occurred to them that Prithviraj was close by. And so Prithviraj, with the consent of his counsellors, decided to steal upon the Turushkas under cover of night and take them by surprise before daybreak. And that is exactly what happened.

Early in the morning the war-drums suddenly rolled and the Rajput archers showered the Afghan camp with thousands of arrows. Before the surprised enemy could recover, the fearful cavalry closed in. The bloodshed was terrible. 'Jay Har Har! In the name of Shiva!' sounded from the yelling mouths of thousands of Rajput warriors, as they slew the Turushkas with sabre, sword and lance. Like the god of death, Prithviraj played havoc among the invaders; holding the reins with his teeth, he wielded a two-edged sabre in each hand. Reserve Rajput forces were ready to attack and as soon as the first wave of cavalry had surged over the Afghan camp it was followed by another wave, so that the Turushkas had no time to recover. Meanwhile the Rajput soldiers who had attacked first had turned their horses and fallen upon the Afghan camp from the opposite side.

Sultan Shihabuddin, horror-struck by the slaughter, shouted at the fleeing Turushkas to stop or he would have them skinned alive, but no one heeded him for this was a matter of life and death. Shihabuddin was terrified. Only a few exhausted and bloody soldiers and body-guards surrounded him now. They did not even have the strength to defend themselves. All of them fell, and Shihabuddin, the once so proud sultan, was taken prisoner and fettered. Victory music was played; drums rolled, flutes, horns and oboes sounded.

King Prithviraj had the captive sultan brought before him, and said: 'You attacked us without declaring war, and have been taught a lesson. Not a single one of your remaining soldiers is fit to wield a sword or draw a bow. Although your life is forfeit to me, I grant it to you. But beware of ever attacking our country again!' He had the sultan seated in an exquisite litter and eight of the best bearers carried him back to his royal seat in Afghanistan. Prithviraj was a noble king, but Sultan Shihabuddin was treacherous and false.

In those days King Bhim of the house of Chalukya sat on the throne of Gurjardhara. He was a good and powerful ruler, but he became jealous and envious when Anangpal handed his kingdom over to Someshvar's son, Prithviraj, for he feared the increasing power of the house of Chauhan. He summoned his counsellors and disclosed his fears to them. 'Tell me what to do,' said Bhim. 'I don't like to see the power of the Chauhans increasing so.'

'You are right,' agreed the counsellors. 'Your eyes see much better and farther than ours. We ought to attack the Chauhans and add a large part of their lands to Gurjardhara.' And so there was a call to arms and the army, equipped with four kinds of weapons, marched towards Delhi.

King Prithviraj was at that time engaged in a military campaign against some rebellious tribes in the north, and had entrusted the government of Delhi to the prudent Kaimas, whom he had brought with him from Ajmer. As soon as Kaimas learned that the Chalukya king, Bhim, was marching on Delhi, he prepared for war, determined to crush the enemy. Someshvar, who had also been warned of Bhim's wicked intentions, set out with his army seeking to destroy the Chalukyan forces before they reached Delhi, and surrounded them. A war to the finish took place. Night had fallen and the swishing of bows and arrows could be heard, while swords and sabres, spears and lances glittered and flashed in the moonlight. The earth was as soaked with blood as if the battle were a bloody sacrifice to the goddess Kali.

At one moment Someshvar noticed that Bhim and his bodyguards were trying to break through the encirclement. He immediately turned his brown horse in that direction and pitched headlong into the most dangerous part of the battle. 'If Bhim falls, we shall win,' he thought. And he rushed towards Bhim, who was dealing blows on all sides. With all the strength he could muster he swung his sabre down on Bhim's neck just above the collar-bone, for that is where the artery is, but the sabre got stuck in Bhim's coat-of-mail and before he could disengage it, the ferocious Bhim with a great blow of his sword cut off his head. The blood of the father who had fought to defend his son spouted high into the air. Everybody was astounded, for King Someshvar had been respected as a noble ruler who had never resorted to trickery. The

Tales Told by the Wanderer in Koregaon

battle was over. A feeling of grief and shame overcame all except King Bhim, who insolently displayed his arrogance.

When the Ajmerian soldiers who had survived the battle with the Chalukyans brought Prithviraj his father's dead body, and told him all that had happened, he was overcome by grief. He made arrangements for an elaborate funeral, and did everything to honour the memory of Someshvar in a befitting manner. For twelve nights he slept on a coarse grass mat and had one simple meal a day. The Ajmerian soldiers were rewarded generously, and the widows and orphans of those who had fallen were granted an annuity for life. Then Prithviraj took over the rule of the Mevat kingdom and united it with the domain he had inherited from his grandfather Anangpal, creating one large realm. The coronation ceremony in Ajmer was modest and unpretentious, for Prithviraj was still mourning his father.

Prithviraj was burning with desire to avenge his father. Bhim's attack had been nothing but mean treachery. All of the Rajput warriors in Delhi and Ajmer shared Prithviraj's feelings in wanting to avenge Someshvar. The war-drums rolled, and Prithviraj's army got ready. And the soldiers were as many as the clouds at the beginning of the rainy season. The heavens resounded with a deafening battle cry coming from five kinds of instruments. Weapons clanged, harness creaked and the elephant-bells jingled. The sergeants and lieutenants gave firm orders, the horses chewed at their bits and pawed the damp earth with their hooves. The standards and the banners fluttered in the southern breeze. The Rajput troops surged forward like herds of enormous elephants bent on destruction from which there is no escape.

The Chalukyan army came in sight with King Bhim at its head. The archers drew their bows, and the other soldiers drew their swords and sabres, firmly grasped their hatchets, lances and spears. The first arrows swished through the air, and the first dead men fell to the ground. The armies clashed, with swords and sabres flashing like lightning. Severed heads rolled on the ground like ripe water-melons and coconuts. The weapons were blunt by now, but the Chauhans made up for this by the force of the blows they struck. King Prithviraj fought like a lion. His whole appearance was terrifying, his eyes glared revengefully, and he felled the Chalukyans as if they were frail stalks of sugar-cane. He shouted encouragement to his soldiers. The battle was as savage as an encounter between the gods and the demons.

How the Brave Prithviraj Defended his Kingdom
and Married Princess Sanyogita

Only a few of the Chalukyan soldiers remained now. Prithviraj pounced upon the desperate King Bhim, knocked the sword out of his hand with a swift blow, and pressing the edge of his sabre to the artery in Bhim's throat, said: 'I've got you, you treacherous villain, you murderer of my father. I have caught you, because I wanted to get my revenge and punish you for your base attack. But I shall honour my father's memory by letting you live and reap the fruit of your foul deeds and your defeat.' He hit Bhim's face with the flat of his sabre and had him fettered and tied to his horse's rump. And that is how he sent him back to the Chalukyan royal seat. Bhim never recovered from this disgrace. Soon afterwards he took to his bed and died. And so Someshvar was avenged.

Sultan Shihabuddin hated the brave Prithviraj so much that the anger the king had aroused in his heart could never disappear. In his spite he resorted to dishonesty, treachery and guile. One day when Prithviraj and his companions were out hunting in the forest near the frontier, the Sultan sent his spies there to find out everything they could. That day Prithviraj had only a few courtiers with him, including of course his faithful friend Chand.

As soon as Sultan Shihabuddin had learnt all he wanted to know he marshalled his soldiers, a hundred times the number of Prithviraj's men, and without difficulty they stealthily encircled the unsuspecting Chauhans. Once they had them trapped, with no hope of escape, Sultan Shihabuddin sent Prithviraj a messenger with the following letter: 'You most villainous of kings! I have never acknowledged your right to the kingdom which Anangpal gave you. I have returned to the land which you consider yours, but my forces are a hundred times stronger than yours and you are trapped. You can't even save yourself by running away like a coward. Now you are my prisoner and as such you will be treated. We two can never come to terms of peace.

Prithviraj read the arrogant note aloud and said: 'Whatever happens, we shall never give up without a fight. No Rajput has ever fled from a battle. This is our land, and as long as any of us live we shall defend it to the last drop of our blood. To arms!'

The Afghan troops closed in on the small group of the Rajputs and the proud Sultan Shihabuddin rode out of the dense jungle on his white stallion, wielding his sabre, ready to strike. He called his soldiers to a halt. Then, certain of his victory, he looked at Prithviraj and laughed

derisively. Without saying a word Prithviraj set five arrows on his bow and shot them all at once. The first arrow landed with a quiver in the Sultan's coat-of-mail precisely where it covered his false heart; the second pierced his white stallion; the third broke his sabre in two; the fourth and the fifth killed two bodyguards standing next to him. Now it was Prithviraj who roared with laughter. Sultan Shihabuddin, who had only been slightly scratched under the coat-of-mail, yelled furiously: 'Charge! Charge!'

And the Afghan troops launched out, a hundred of them to each of Prithviraj's men. Suddenly the poet Chand whispered the magic formula and immediately fifty-two miraculous warriors appeared before him: 'What do you command, sir?' Chand replied: 'We are being overpowered, please help us!'

The Rajput men wielded their swords and sabres, fighting like lions, but the fifty-two warriors gave them invaluable support. Every one of them suddenly had fifty-two hands, each of which carried a weapon — a sword, sabre, lance, spear, dagger, club or a hatchet. They caused terrible bloodshed to the Afghan army. The horrified Shihabuddin turned his horse and like a skunk who had been driven from the hen-house by the farmer, fled to the Afghan frontier, cursing all the way. He was the only Turushka to return alive. The rest were dead on the battle-field, left to be devoured by beasts of prey.

Years passed, the old king of Kannauj, Vijaypal, had joined his ancestors and his kingdom was ruled by his son Jaychand, who watched Prithviraj's growth of power with displeasure, although they were cousins. 'He makes me feel bitter and resentful. We ought to prevent him becoming so powerful...' said Jaychand to his counsellor.

The counsellor replied: 'You are certainly right, Your Majesty, but a military campaign might result in failure, defeat and confusion in the kingdom. If you really intend to attack Prithviraj, you should first arrange the marriage of your daughter, Princess Sanyogita; once you have provided for her, you can unsheathe the sword and wage a war without misgivings about her future.'

'Well said,' agreed Jaychand. He summoned his daughter and said: 'Dear child, the time has come for you to be wed. According to the ancient Indian custom I shall invite all the eligible suitors and you will choose one of them for your husband. Then we shall arrange a wedding. Consider carefully whom you will choose.'

Princess Sanyogita answered: 'It is not necessary to invite all the kings and princes, for I have already chosen Prithviraj of the house of Chauhan.' This made Jaychand very angry and he grew cross with his daughter. But Sanyogita insisted: 'Father, surely you wouldn't want me to marry one of those rabbits who have to pay you taxes and gain your permission for anything they want to do? According to ancient custom I have the right to choose the husband I want, and you mustn't force me or persuade me to do otherwise.'

Jaychand shouted furiously: 'You will obey me and do as I wish!'

'Not this time, father,' said Sanyogita firmly. 'I will obey in anything but this. I would rather be dead in the sacred waters of the Ganges than be touched by the hand of any of your henchmen, who are so proud of their noble blood, but do not care that their minds are base. I am the daughter of a king and only the king of my heart can be my husband. It's either Prithviraj, or no one!'

Jaychand realized that he must act quickly, firmly and with determination. He imprisoned his disobedient daughter and her nurse in a fortress on the bank of the river Ganges, and immediately sent messengers to the neighbouring kings, inviting them to the ceremony in which Sanyogita was to choose her husband. He was hoping to make her give in. But he did not invite Prithviraj, the king of Delhi.

Meanwhile in prison, Sanyogita wondered what to do. She loved Prithviraj and did not want any other husband. One day she was walking in the garden, which was surrounded by high walls and guarded by sentries. Deep in thought, she sat down by the pool and watching the many water-fowls she said to herself: 'I wish I had wings! Then I could fly to Delhi and I am sure Prithviraj would agree that I have the right to choose the man I love for my husband.' Suddenly she had an idea...

She saw a golden swan swimming on the pool and she addressed it: 'Dear swan, would you like to do me a favour?' The swan answered: 'Yes I would, Your Royal Highness — what do you want me to do?'

Sanyogita said: 'Dear swan, since the walls and the sentries are no obstacle for you, please fly to Delhi and tell King Prithviraj that my father Jaychand has imprisoned me in this fortress, and that he is arranging a ceremony during which I am supposed to choose one of his vassal kings for my husband. But Prithviraj Chauhan is the only man I want for a husband. Tell him to hasten and set me free, or I will be forced to end my young life by fire, rope, poison, water or a sharp two-edged dagger.'

'It will be my pleasure to do this for you,' said the golden swan, and spreading its wings it soared up and vanished in the distance.

King Prithviraj was sitting in his garden, playing a lute beneath a flowering shrub. All at once he heard the rustle of glittering wings as the golden swan landed on the lawn in front of him and spoke in a human voice: 'Hail, oh king! The lovely princess Sanyogita has sent me to you. Her father, Jaychand, has imprisoned her in his fortress on the bank of the Ganges, and wants to marry her to a suitor of his choice. But she loves you, for you are a tiger among kings, and a bull among men, and you are the one she desires and yearns for. She begs you to help her, and to spoil Jaychand's plans.'

'This must have been ordained by the gods,' thought Prithviraj, and thanking the swan he sent it back to tell Sanyogita that she could rely on his help. For he had admired the Kannauj princess for a long time, but had not dared to ask for her hand for fear of being refused by her, and also because he was aware that Jaychand disliked him. He hurried to his friend Chand and when he had told him everything, he asked: 'What do you think I should do to spoil Jaychand's wicked plans and make everything turn out well?'

Chand thought awhile and then he said: 'King Jaychand is not being fair. He is too stern to his daughter, and what is more, he has invited only the suitors he likes — fawning flatterers all of them. We'll teach him a lesson, but we'll do it openly and honestly. I suggest you do this, Your Majesty: send your spies to find out the day and the hour of the ceremony. We'll go there when the time comes. Although we will come uninvited, it will be no offence, since you have the right to visit your cousin whenever you like. If Princess Sanyogita really loves you, she will choose you and no one will be able to object.' Prithviraj agreed to do as Chand had so wisely advised him. Jaychand had no idea what was in store for him.

Meanwhile in Kannauj there were great preparations for the splendid ceremony. The whole city was decorated with flags, banners, flowers, wreaths, precious fabrics from afar and with Kashmir and Persian carpets. It was a wonderful sight, worthy of the glorious event. Guests from all directions began to flow into Kannauj; not only kings, princes, rulers, potentates and nobles; but also stall-keepers, entertainers, snake-charmers, jugglers, tight-rope walkers, musicians, dancers, actors and actresses, pick-pockets, impostors and thieves of all kinds.

The day before the gala choosing-ceremony Jaychand sent eight bearers with a beautiful litter, accompanied by the royal guard, to fetch Sanyogita. He was quite sure everything would go according to his wishes. Prithviraj and Chand were already in Kannauj and had taken lodgings in a roadside inn, disguised as wayfarers, so that Jaychand should not find out about them. Princess Sanyogita did not know what Prithviraj intended to do and her heart trembled with fear. But she trusted the king of Delhi and hoped all would end well.

When the long-awaited moment arrived, determined by the astrologers according to Sanyogita's horoscope, all the kings and rulers, and also Jaychand and his courtiers were already assembled in the throne-room. King Jaychand gave the sign for Princess Sanyogita and her maidens to appear. The room hummed with expectation and curiosity. Each of the suitors hoped to be the one Sanyogita would choose for her husband, for they knew Prithviraj was not present and some had even been informed that Jaychand had not invited him. Also, Jaychand was spiteful and wanted to humiliate his daughter and to punish her for her pride; so he had a clay statue of King Prithviraj made and dressed as a servant, which he put at the entrance of the throne-room as if it were a door-keeper. It was a base insult.

The maidens entered, with Sanyogita in the midst of them. All the kings, princes and nobles hailed them and bowed to the lovely princess, who took no heed of them, as her eyes were searching for her beloved, the man she had decided to choose. She was confused, since she could not see Prithviraj anywhere, and her heart grew cold with fear. When she noticed the offensive statue at the door, her eyes filled with tears and she was ashamed of her own father. But she controlled her feelings and in her heart of hearts she was firmly decided. 'Oh no, father,' she thought, 'this is no way to make me change my mind. I have never been persuaded by force or compulsion, and never will be!'

From the hands of the sacrificial priest she received a gorgeous wreath, which she was to place round the neck of the one she chose of her own free will to be her husband. Walking slowly towards Prithviraj's statue, she put the wreath round its neck. Everyone was astounded. King Jaychand was about to start shouting in his fury, when suddenly both parts of the door flew wide-open, and there stood Prithviraj with his friend Chand.

'Good evening, my royal cousin,' he said to Jaychand. 'And good evening to all of you, gentlemen. My compliments to you, oh proud and lovely Sanyogita, who are my wife now!'

Jaychand sprang from the throne, his face red with anger. He cried: 'What is the meaning of this? What's going on? What do you want here?'

'You all saw that Sanyogita chose me for her husband although, cousin, you forgot to invite me — not intentionally, I hope,' said Prithviraj.

'This doesn't count!' said Jaychand, gasping for breath.

'Oh yes it does,' retorted the poet Chand firmly. 'Just you remember what the law says, if you haven't forgotten all they taught you when you were young.'

'You impertinent fellow!' Jaychand drew his sabre. 'Get them! Save my daughter!' And they all rushed at them. Prithviraj, Sanyogita and Chand quickly backed away and, slamming the door behind them, ran to the courtyard where two nimble-footed stallions were waiting for them. They immediately mounted them and darted through the gate. Sabre in hand, with the rejected suitors at his heels, the enraged Jaychand dashed out of the palace yelling in a croaking voice: 'Close the gates! Don't let them out!' But by then Prithviraj, Sanyogita, and Chand were far away. When Jaychand realized that he was powerless to do anything, he stuck his sabre, which was useless to him now, into the ground right up to the hilt. Then he had the sentries, who had been guarding the gates, flogged until they bled. But it was all of no use. The guests departed hastily, leaving Jaychand alone with his gloomy thoughts.

In the meantime, three riders on two nimble-footed stallions were hurrying up the dusty road to Delhi, their hearts filled with joy and happiness.

When they came to Delhi, King Prithviraj married Princess Sanyogita, and so his kingdom acquired the loveliest of queens.

The moon slowly travelled among the stars in the sky. The wandering story-teller picked up his iktar, played a little tune and sang:

'Though the story seems a lie
Truth is hidden from the eye.
What's a lie and what is true?
Make a guess, it's up to you.'

And he began another story.

The Greedy Pupil

In ancient times holy men and sages used to dwell in hermitages in the forest, where they meditated in peace and quiet, and taught their pupils various sciences, doctrines of philosophy, astronomy, astrology, the grammar of the classical language, and many other things. The surrounding woods afforded plenty of excellent fruit and it was quite usual for one of the pupils to go begging for food in the neighbouring villages.

Long ago one of these hermitages was inhabited by the sage Vishvanath. He had a single pupil, whose name was Chunda. He was a slovenly, lazy and disobedient boy, and in addition he was a hearty eater.

One day his master Vishvanath said to him: 'You are unusually inattentive and careless today, Chunda! You'd better go begging in the village.' Chunda picked up a basket and, taking his time, walked to the village. There he went from door to door, and everywhere they gave him one or two pies. When the basket was full, Chunda decided to go back. But on his way out of the village he sat down to count the pies under a spreading fig-tree.

There were thirty-two of them, all sweet-smelling and delicious-looking. Chunda felt his mouth water and thought: 'Master Vishvanath is kind and fair. When I get back he is sure to give me half the pies — that means sixteen of them. Why shouldn't I eat them here now when I'm so hungry?' And he ate sixteen pies with relish.

Then he picked up the basket and slowly sauntered towards the forest. He could not take his mind off the delicious pies and continued to think: 'If I bring sixteen pies to the hermitage, Master Vishvanath is sure to give me eight of them. Why shouldn't I eat them straight away? I will!' And he did.

Now he had eight pies in the basket, and his thoughts continued: 'When Master Vishvanath sees that I have brought eight pies, he will certainly let me have four. I'm as sure of that as I'm sure my appetite is great!' And he ate another four pies.

And since his thoughts of the delicious pies and his kind master Vishvanath, who always shared things fairly, did not forsake him, Chunda ate two more pies, then another one, so that now there was only one single pie left in the basket.

'Master Vishvanath is sure to share it with me,' said Chunda to himself, 'and will give me half of the pie. So I'll eat my half right now!' And so he did.

When he arrived at the hermitage with only half a pie, Vishvanath wrung his hands in exasperation and exclaimed: 'Is that all they gave you in the whole village? Half a pie?'

Chunda, who did not dare to lie, admitted everything and told him how he had gradually eaten one pie after another.

Master Vishvanath was shocked and shouted angrily: 'You greedy boy! You glutton! How could you ever manage to eat so many pies?'

'Like this,' said Chunda calmly, and reaching for the remaining bit he put it in his mouth and swallowed it.

The wandering story-teller came to the end of the story and all his listeners went away laughing. Jagannath the story-teller went home with his friend Jagannath the farmer. The farmer's wife made them some tea and when they had drunk it and chattered a little, they went to bed.

In the morning when they got up, and after bathing near the well, they had pancakes and tea with buffalo's milk for breakfast. Then they said goodbye, and the wandering story-teller set out for the next village, Kadas.

As everywhere else, the villagers here greeted him joyfully and treated him to all they could offer in their poverty. Then they all gathered on the open space in front of the little temple of the Ape-god Hanuman, and Jagannath began his story.

Of the Parting and Reunion of Prince Dhola and Princess Maru

King Pingal ruled the kingdom of Pugal, and King Nal ruled the kingdom of Narvar. They had never met, but suddenly fate brought them together. When a terrible plague broke out in the land of Pugal, King Pingal, fearing death, fled with his family to Narvar and begged King Nal for refuge. King Nal received him with all the honour due to a ruler, and gave him a palace, horses, servants and all other appropriate things.

The king of Narvar had a son named Dhola — a handsome boy of good bearing. And Maru, King Pingal's daughter, was the most charming young lady. When the queen of Pugal saw them talking together, in the royal gardens, she said: 'Surely they were meant for each other! They belong together!'

'Hush, madam,' retorted King Pingal. 'This is no time to think of that kind of thing. You know how pitiful our situation is. If we wanted to marry our daughter now, we would be the laughing-stock of the whole court.'

'Can a cuckoo live without the mango-tree? Or a frog without a pond? Don't make the mistake of delaying things for too long, my dear royal husband!' persisted the queen.

Knowing his wife, King Pingal waved a hand and said condescendingly: 'Do as you think best.'

'I dare say it's all settled,' thought the queen of Pugal, and went off to put her idea into practice. And as she knew how to arrange things according to her wishes, the glorious wedding of Princess Maru and Prince Dhola actually did take place very soon. Everyone was happy, and the festivities and rejoicing were endless.

When the plague in Pugal was over, King Pingal and his family returned home. Since Princess Maru was still too young, she did not stay with her husband, Dhola, but went to Pugal with her parents. Dhola felt lonely and missed his wife as much as she missed him.

Princess Maru was so beautiful! She walked like a golden swan, her legs were like the stems of a banana-tree, she was as slim in the waist as a young lioness, her face was like the heavenly moon, her eyes were like those of a finch and her voice as mellow as the lute. Sitting by the window with her head resting on her hands, she watched the distant horizon, thinking of Dhola all the time. Clouds of the darkest colours were gathering there, for the rainy season was about to come, and thunder sounded in the distance. Maru thought of her husband, who was so far away, and her eyes filled with tears.

'Why are you so sad today? What sorrow troubles your soul?' asked her companions.

'My husband is far away in Narvar, and I am here. I can't think of anything else; he is the master of my mind, and even in my dreams I see only him,' complained Maru, and her companions did not know how to help her. Maru cried bitterly, and so her companions hurried to tell the queen how sad the princess was.

The next morning the queen visited King Pingal, and said: 'Listen, my dear royal husband, to what I am going to tell you: our daughter Maru is suffering because she misses her husband. She is unhappy and weeps all the time. What are you going to do about it?'

'I'll send a messenger to Narvar,' replied the king without hesitation, 'and ask Dhola to come for his bride. That's what I'll do!'

And indeed he did. But Dhola did not arrive, nor did he answer the message. King Pingal sent several other messengers, but the result was the same as if he had done nothing at all. No one knew what was going on, and Maru was dying of sorrow.

One day a merchant dealing in splendid horses of various breeds — the Arabs, Persians and the Turks, and their crossbreeds, as well as mustangs and domestic and Afghan ponies — came to Pugal. King Pingal invited him to his palace and chose a couple of fine horses for his stables. Then he gave the merchant a rich reward and talked to him about the countries which the merchant had visited on his business trips. While they were talking, the merchant saw Princess Maru, pale as the crescent of the autumn moon, but nevertheless charming and beautiful.

'Who was the beautiful princess I saw when I was talking to the king?' he asked the groom, casually.

'That is King Pingal's only daughter,' answered the groom. 'When she was very young, she married Dhola, the prince of Narvar, but he has not come for her, although she is now grown-up, and the king has sent him several letters of invitation.'

The merchant begged permission to see the king again, and when it was granted and the king asked him what his wish was, the merchant said: 'Not long ago I visited Narvar, Your Majesty, and I think I know why Prince Dhola has not answered your letters.'

'Tell me all about it,' said the king.

'I sold a lot of horses there,' began the merchant, 'and I stayed at the royal court of Narvar for several days. I know that Dhola has married the daughter of the king of Malva; her name is Malvani, and she is extremely jealous. No doubt that is the reason why Dhola has not answered your messages. Malvani has placed her men — most of them rogues — on all roads leading to Narvar, and no letter that might in any way endanger her plans can ever reach the hands of the king or Prince Dhola. I came to know Dhola well during my visit there. He is a noble and just man.'

King Pingal said to the merchant: 'You have explained a lot. Take this ring, and be sure that whenever you visit my kingdom again, whether it be my royal seat or my court, you will always be welcome.' The merchant thanked him, bowed, and left. Then the king summoned the sacrificial priest and commanded: 'Go and fetch Dhola, the prince of Narvar, holy man.' The sacrificial priest clasped his hands before his brow and went.

But the queen said: 'My dear royal husband, do you really think that this will work? If Malvani is as cunning as the merchant said she is, then not even a whole monastery of holy men can ever deceive her. You would do much better to send minstrels to Narvar — as many as you can find. They are the ones to arouse longing for a distant wife or mistress, not the priests!'

And so the king summoned all the minstrels at the royal seat and in the vicinity of the castle. When they arrived, he presented them with gold coins and said to them: 'I want you to go to Narvar and bring Prince Dhola here. How you do it is your business. But if you succeed, I will show my gratitude most generously.'

When the minstrels left the king, Maru called them and full of hope and joy asked: 'When are you setting out on your long and arduous journey — tonight or tomorrow?'

The minstrels replied: 'We will leave tonight. If we stay alive, we shall return. If we perish on the way, we'll remain there.'

'The Narvar country is beautiful,' said the princess. 'When you get there, please give Prince Dhola, my dearest husband, a message from me.' And she continued: 'A good messenger can make a wish come true by delivering a message well. A good messenger can bring me my husband from distant Narvar. Dear bards, tell Dhola that his wife, whom he wedded at the sacred fire long ago, yearns to see him again. And also tell him this: that his wife's heart does not dwell in her body any more. It has fled from her to be near him, and that he should bring it back to her, like the beater who brings back the shy elephant. That the rich canopy of her youth is ready to shade him while he rests. The lotus-flower of her youth is in blossom; that he should come and suck its nectar, sweet bumble-bee!'

The minstrels remembered the message, and immediately set out on the journey. They safely crossed the mountains and the desert, and were only a few miles from the boundaries of Narvar when they were halted by ominous-looking armed men. These were Princess Malvani's henchmen. 'Who are you, and where are you going?' they questioned the minstrels. 'Do you bring any letters or messages? Speak or you'll have a bad time!'

'We are poor wandering people who earn our living by singing,' replied the minstrels. 'We do not have any letters. You can look if you like. Who would ask wanderers like us to deliver messages?'

'Be off then you rabble!' said the commander, and he let them pass. The minstrels did not show how happy they were, but went. Soon they came to the royal seat of Narvar. They pitched their tents in front of the royal palace, just below Prince Dhola's windows. And in the evening, when the day's commotion and bustle had subsided, they began to sing:

'Narvar and Pugal quite far apart lie,

Yet love is a tie; so why be sad, why?

For Dhola is here and Maru is there...

It seems that the prince for his bride doesn't care.'

This and other songs of the same kind sounded the whole night through. Dhola heard them, and in the morning he rose as if in a fever, feeling downcast and as weak as a once-so-speedy fish left on a dry bank in the summer drought. As soon as the sun rose he walked out of the palace, straight to the minstrels, and addressed them: 'Where do you come from? What is the meaning of your song?'

'We come from Pugal', they replied. 'It is King Pingal and his daughter Maru who sent us to you, oh Prince. Maru, the charming fairy-like maiden is your wife since you were children, but you have forgotten her. King Pingal has sent you several letters, and you have never replied.'

'I never received a single letter from King Pingal!' exclaimed Dhola. 'None of his messengers ever reached me.'

'Now, at last, we have come,' said the minstrels. 'Listen to the message from Princess Maru.' And they delivered the whole message, word for word.

'If only my heart were a falcon! If only I had wings!' thought Dhola, who began to feel a longing for his forgotten bride. He rewarded the minstrels with gold and precious stones, and returned to the palace, determined to leave immediately for the kingdom of Pugal.

But Malvani observed that something had happened. 'My husband has changed since yesterday,' she thought. 'Whatever has happened, I must find out!' and putting her arms round Dhola's neck, she said endearingly: 'My dear master and husband, you haven't spoken or smiled at me lately, as if you were angry with me. You look confused. What's worrying you? Tell me. Perhaps I may help you.'

'My dear, soft-eyed wife, I want to go away for some time,' said Dhola, hesitatingly.

'Do you prefer to visit foreign lands although you are master of the splendid castle of Narvar and have a devoted wife and all your heart may desire?'

'Listen, my beauty,' said Dhola, 'I will tell you the truth: I long to see my first wife, Maru.' Without saying a word Malvani fell on the ground, as if she had been bitten by a snake. Dhola sprinkled cold water over her face and fanned her until she regained consciousness. He did all he could, but there seemed to be nothing he could soothe her with, and there was no end to her tears.

'Stay at home. Don't go away!' begged Malvani. 'Don't forsake me!'

'I want to go, and I will!' said Dhola firmly.

'If you must drive a dagger in my heart,' said Malvani, 'please go away when I am sleeping, so that I won't see you leaving me.'

'I promise you that,' said Dhola, and he called to the groom: 'Hey, prepare the best and fastest camel!'

The groom went to the stables, and picked a sturdy camel — a king among the camels — that had been fed on betel leaves and had drunk water from the Ganges. Dhola took a good look at it and wondered: 'Is this the right camel to bridle? Am I to put the bells on it?'

And the camel answered: 'Yes, I am the right camel. Don't worry, bridle me, and put the bells on me. I am the camel you want. And if I don't get you to Pugal in one day and one night, then I was never born of a mother-camel!'

'That's excellent!' thought Dhola, and started to prepare for the long journey. But he could not leave Narvar because he had promised Malvani to leave when she was asleep, and Malvani was wide-awake for fourteen days and nights. Only then, completely exhausted, did she fall into a deep slumber. Dhola quickly had the camel brought and saddled, and with his own hands fastened the bells onto the harness. Then he mounted the camel and, gripping the reins firmly, he spurred it: 'To Pugal! To Pugal!'

Malvani heard the camel snorting, and woke up. She rushed to the window only to see Dhola riding out of the gate. Crying and screaming, she ran to the yard. There she bent down, filled her hands with sand,

and said: 'Only his footprints are here. That is all he has left me. My joy, my wealth, my youth, my everything is gone! Oh! My darling has wounded me as cruelly as if he had stabbed me with a chiselled Churason sword!'

While Malvani was sadly weeping, Dhola happily rode on to Pugal. When he had crossed the Adavalarau mountains, he jumped off the camel, led it to a little pool, and said: 'Take your fill of water and fodder because from here on lies the parched desert. The water in the pool is fresh and sweet, but you'll have to make do with thistles and thorny bushes for food. There is no hope of finding betel leaves in this desert, although that is the only fodder worthy of your noble muzzle.'

As Dhola was talking to the camel, a strolling artist approached them on the road from Pugal. It was plain from his goggling eyes and jerky movements that he was mad. His words confirmed it.

The artist addressed Dhola: 'Hah! You becamelled rider! You're having a pleasant trip on your cosy saddle, curse your mother! And here am I, left to drag my way through the desert on my own, carrying my water-bag and a few flat-cakes on my back. For I don't mean to leave my old bones lying somewhere behind a sand-dune yet, I swear to Shiva!'

Dhola took no notice of him. But the man continued: 'I see you're going to Pugal. Curse your mother! A fine city that is! I'm glad to be out of it. It was sheer luck I didn't end up in the royal prison there, hang them all! Hah!'

Dhola's curiosity was aroused: 'What happened to you in Pugal?'

'I'll never tell anyone, not even you,' answered the madman. 'I'll be damned! If it weren't for the ugly old princess who pleaded for me with her royal dad, I'd be rotting now in a stinking cell, somewhere deep down under the fortress. Hah!'

'Which princess are you talking about, you fool?' exclaimed Dhola.

'They only have one there. Her name is Maru. They say she is married to a prince from over there,' and the madman pointed in the direction of Narvar, 'but he has forgotten all about her, and she is dried up with grief like last year's apricot.'

Dhola could not believe his ears.

'Well, I'll be on my way. You don't travel as fast on foot as on a camel, I swear to Shiva!' said he, and plodded on through the desert.

Dhola stood there like a tree-trunk twisted by lightning. His mind was heavy with gloomy thoughts. 'Well, camel, what shall we do now? We have come this far to find out that it was all in vain. I have a mind to go back at once.' And taking hold of the reins, he was about to head for Narvar.

'Don't be rash, prince,' said the camel. 'Never trust the word of a madman. What if all he said isn't true? Did he prove anything? Look, there's a minstrel coming over there. Ask him. Minstrels are usually wise, and they never lie.'

Dhola considered this a good idea, and turned to the minstrel: 'I am Dhola, the prince of Narvar. I heard that Princess Maru has grown old and ugly. Tell me the truth, I want to know whether to continue my journey or go back home.'

The minstrel said: 'I know your story. I also know the princess of Pugal. Your Highness is only a little older; look at yourself — have you grown old? Then why should she have grown old? I saw her recently and I can confirm that she has never been more beautiful than she is now.'

'Tell me all about her,' said Dhola.

'Maru moves with the grace of the waves of the Ganges, she is as wise as the goddess Sarasvati and her heart is the kindest in the world. She is patient, virtuous and gentle. She walks like the golden swan, her waist is as slim as a wasp's and her voice is as sweet as a cuckoo's song. Her eyes are almond-shaped and on her brow a brilliant jewel shines like a butterfly sitting on a water-lily.'

Dhola interrupted him: 'And what else? What else?'

The minstrel smiled: 'Maru possesses as many virtues as there are stars in the heavens, and you want me to tell you all about her in one breath. I only have one mouth and one tongue, you impatient young man!' And he continued with his description of the princess of Pugal. When he had finished, Dhola gave him a handful of gold coins and bade him farewell. Then he continued on his journey, impatient and eager to see Maru.

After a while he said to the camel: 'It's still a long way to Pugal. Do you remember what you promised me? I doubt whether you will keep your promise. We're hardly half-way.'

'Don't hit me on the back, master,' replied the camel. 'Don't press me with your legs so hard, and loosen the bridle. But tighten my girth,

and if I don't keep the promise I made in Narvar, then I was never born of a mother-camel.' Dhola did as the camel said, and they rode on even faster.

While they were passing through the desert lands, Princess Maru felt strangely excited. She said to her companions: 'Something is happening to me. I don't know what it is, but I'm trembling all over; my eyelids, my hands, my lips... I'm suddenly happy and full of joy, and I don't know why. But I can guess; I think I know. My husband, whom I have not seen since I was a child, is coming to our city! That's what it must be!'

And indeed, Dhola was approaching the royal seat of Pugal. His camel had kept its promise, and they were already at the gate of the royal palace. Dhola told the sentries who he was, and King Pingal came to meet him and welcome him most kindly. He took Dhola to his chambers, and sent the servants for the princess.

Maru was overwhelmed with joy. 'Oh, my dearest friends,' she cried, 'I knew it! My husband and master has come! All my wishes have come true in a single day. Today is the day of love, today is a gay and glorious day! I see joy everywhere: my mirror is smiling, the colonnade is dancing, my bed is springing up and down, the chest is shaking, the carpet is waving, the candle-stick is skipping and the door is opening of its own accord.'

Her companions bathed the princess in a bath of scented foam, they cleaned all seven openings of the body, rubbed her with rare ointments, combed her long hair into a braid and lastly dressed her in a lovely embroidered gown. Then they accompanied her to the chambers which King Pingal let Dhola use during his stay in Pugal.

When Dhola saw Maru he thought: 'How beautiful she has become! Is that the glow of lightning, or is her smile so bright?'

They greeted each other shyly. Dhola took Maru by the hand and said: 'Come and sit down, my charming wife, we have a lot to talk about...' They sat down on a low bed, covered with soft carpets and furskins.

'Tell me,' said Dhola, 'How have you kept so fresh and young all the long time we were apart? Why is it that you are even more beautiful than when I last saw you?'

'It is because you have come,' answered Maru. 'Even the frog, listless and weary during the drought, becomes lively and young as soon as the clouds open and pour their water on the earth.'

Her words pleased Dhola very much. He bent to her and kissed her gently. Maru put her arms round him. They had been away from each other for such a long time! Long had the dry desert been lying between them, long had the cruel Adavalarau range been standing between them. Now they were together, inseparable as the water-lily and the playful bumble-bee, as the river Ganges and the ocean, as the liana and the sandal-tree.

Dhola, prince of Narvar, stayed at his father-in-law's royal palace a whole fortnight. And all the time there was singing, dancing, music, merry-making and entertainment.

When Dhola and Maru were getting ready for the journey to Narvar, King Pingal gave his daughter a rich dowry: golden jewels, precious stones, elephants, horses, slaves and also a maiden light-bearer. It was her duty to take care of the candles and the oil-lamps, to cut the wicks in time, to add oil, and when it was dark to carry a light for the princess wherever she went. And because there were rumours of the desert being full of robbers, he added a hundred brave soldiers for their protection.

The great caravan did not travel as fast as Dhola, speeding on his camel from Narvar. They were still on their way the second day and had not even gone half the distance. In the evening they camped in a deserted place, but close to a well with sweet water. Dhola pitched a tent for Maru and himself, and the caravan lay down to sleep. Only the guards kept watch.

During the night, when Dhola and his pretty wife were fast asleep, the malicious, long, spotted serpent Pivnau crawled into the tent. It put its huge jaws to Princess Maru's face and greedily sucked her sweet breath, making Maru breathe its foul and poisonous stench. It stayed in the tent until sunrise and then vanished without anyone noticing it.

Dawn came, the horizon grew pale, the horses began to neigh, the camels snorted. Dhola woke up and kissed his wife's white brow. It was cold as marble! He tried to wake her up, calling her name, but it was of no avail. The maiden light-bearer came in, and as soon as she looked at Maru's pale face she ran out in horror, crying: 'Alas! Alas! Maru is dead! The serpent Pivnau has sucked her breath away!' Everyone crowded round the tent, weeping and wailing. Dhola was desperate.

To those who were trying to console him he said: 'Your kind words are of no use, for Maru is dead. I don't want to hear them. Go back to Pugal, or go wherever you wish, just leave me alone.' And so the whole caravan dispersed in various directions and Dhola was left alone, holding his wife's dead body in his arms. His camel stood watching him with sad eyes.

'Oh, Maru, Maru,' groaned Dhola. 'It is all my fault! Why didn't I stay awake and protect you! Your life was slowly dying away, like the light of an oil-lamp, and I did nothing to prevent it. My heart is ready to break with sorrow!' After a while he gently laid poor Maru in the shadow and began piling up wood for a funeral pyre. In his despair he talked to Maru as if she were alive: 'Life in this world has lost its meaning. I shall enter the fire with you and we will die together.'

Suddenly, on the path leading to the camp, appeared a thin holy man, a member of the Brotherhood of the Left Hand, accompanied by a young woman of the same faith. He overheard Dhola's last words and said: 'Who ever heard of a man being burned alive with the corpse of his wife? It's only the women who, since ancient days, have chosen to die in the fire rather than lead the life of widows. Do you want to die for nothing?'

'That's my own business,' replied Dhola, 'not yours. Go your way and leave me to make my own decisions.'

'That is the princess of Pugal, Maru,' said the holy man's companion. 'I know her. And you, holy man, since you know the art of all-powerful magic, must bring her back to life.'

'I don't have to do anything, you foolish woman,' grunted the holy man. 'Do you think the difference between life and death is so important? Doesn't that of which man is made outlast him even after death, only in a different form and elsewhere?'

'Bring her back to life, or I'll go to the pyre with her!'

'You can't do that!' exclaimed the holy man. 'How could I perform my rituals without you? You mustn't die!'

'Do you think the difference between life and death is so important?' said the woman mocking him. 'Doesn't that of which man is made outlast him even after death?'

Without saying another word, the holy man turned to Maru, and murmuring a magic formula first touched her brow and then, taking some balm from a silver jar, rubbed it on her lips. Maru quivered, sighed, opened her eyes, sat up, and looked around in amazement.

'What happened to me? I was so far away.' Dhola took her in his arms and told her everything. Then he offered the holy man a reward, but the latter said: 'Keep your riches, prince, I have no use for them, for true knowledge is the greatest of all values. And that I possess. I will only accept this emerald ring from you, as I need it for performing my magic.' And he walked away with his companion up the narrow path leading into the desert.

'Since everything has turned out so well,' said Dhola laughing, 'let's both mount my camel, and we'll be in Narvar in no time.'

But now there was the sound of horses' hooves in the distance, and a group of riders appeared on the horizon, followed by camels carrying women and luggage. Their leader rode up to Dhola: 'What's the hurry, sir? Why don't you sit down with us for a while; we'll have something to eat and drink, and then we can travel to Narvar together, for we too are going there.'

Neither Dhola nor Maru suspected that these were desert robbers, and that their leader was the infamous Umar, a villain, blackguard and cut-throat. Both accepted Umar's invitation. Dhola tied his camel's front feet to keep it from straying, and Maru and he sat down with the robbers.

Among the robbers' wives there was one who used to serve at the royal palace in Pugal, and she recognized Princess Maru at once. She felt sorry for her and the prince, and decided to upset Umar's plans, and save the royal couple. And so, walking past them as if by chance, she sang softly:

'While you both are drinking, eating,
And your camel feeds,
Evil men plot to destroy you
By their cruel deeds.
Of the victims caught by robbers
Few have ever fled...
The young wife will be stolen by them,
The husband will be dead.
If your husband, Maru,
And your life you cherish,
Go and hit the camel hard
Or you both must perish!'

Nobody took any notice of her song, not even Dhola who was talking to the robbers without the faintest suspicion. Only Maru heard it. She stood up, walked over to the camel, and hit it with a stick. The camel cried out in pain and injury.

'Your camel is calling you,' said Umar to Dhola. 'Go and calm it.'

Dhola went to the camel, where Maru was waiting for him impatiently. She whispered: 'Those are the desert robbers, and their leader is Umar! We must run away, or evil will befall us!'

They both mounted the camel quickly, and Dhola spurred it. But alas! He had forgotten that the camel's front feet were tied together. Nothing could be done now, because Umar and his robbers had noticed their flight and were pursuing them on their horses. The camel, in spite of having its feet bound, ran like the wind. After a while they saw a beggar walking towards them. He was one of Umar's spies, who informed him when and where it would be profitable to commit a theft or a robbery. But luckily, he was otherwise a feeble-minded man. Dhola threw him a knife and ordered: 'Quickly, cut the rope which is tied round the camel's feet! You can keep the knife as a reward. And tell Umar how you helped us.' Now the camel ran twice as fast.

The pursuers met the beggar a little later, and gathered around him. 'Which way did the fugitives on a camel with bound feet go?' shouted Umar.

The beggar replied: 'Only Prince Dhola with his wife passed this way. I cut the rope that tied the camel's feet to help it run better. I think they went to Narvar.'

'You fool!' cried Umar, hitting the beggar with the flat of his sabre. He ground his teeth and rolled his eyes: 'You helped them! Now we'll never catch them! I'll punish you for this!' The robbers had to return empty-handed.

Dhola and his charming wife happily arrived at the royal seat of the kingdom of Narvar. King Nal and his wife Champavati welcomed both their son and his wife most heartily and arranged a splendid feast. Malvani came too, and she was so happy to see Dhola again that she did not even object to the presence of Princess Maru. Soon Dhola's wives became friends, and there never were two companions as devoted as Malvani and Maru.

The one was like a jasmine blossom, the other like the flower of the mango. And Dhola was their bumble-bee.

The listeners sat in silence, their minds' dwelling on the story of the prince of Narvar and the princess of Pugal. The wandering story-teller picked up his iktar, played a little tune and then sang:

'Though the story seems a lie
Truth is hidden from the eye.
What's a lie and what is true?
Make a guess, it's up to you.'

And he began another story.

Tales Told by the Wanderer in Kadas

The Election of the King of the Birds

Once upon a time, in the days when the birds did not have their own king, they met to discuss the question of electing a just ruler. After long deliberation they agreed to elect the owl, because he was the wisest of all birds. But at this point the humming-bird whistled and said: 'We forgot to invite the crow! The election will not be valid. I'll go and fetch her.' And he flew off.

When he returned with the crow she said: 'A fine king you have chosen, indeed! Aren't there any other birds than owls? What about swans, nightingales, eagles? Do you really want the bad-tempered owl to be your king? Take a good look at him. His beak is hideously curved, he keeps his eyes shut all the time, as if he were planning some treachery. He is cruel and vulgar by nature. But he is not a bit cunning and therefore would be no good as a king. You know well that the weak have often escaped the stronger by cunning.'

'How did that happen?' asked the birds.

And the crow began...

A couple of crows nested on a tree. Whenever the hen laid eggs a cobra crawled out of the hollow tree-trunk and ate them. The crows were very unhappy, but they could not fight the cobra. One day they complained to their friend the jackal, who often feasted on carcasses with them, and he suggested: 'The only way to fight a stronger enemy is by cunning. That's what the clever crab did to the greedy heron.'

'How did that happen?' asked the crows.

And the jackal told them...

There was an old heron living on the shore of a lake. He was weak and sickly, and not too good at catching fish any more. So he stood at the water's edge, lifted his long beak and wailed loudly. The fish, their curiosity aroused, swam up to him and asked: 'Why are you crying?' The heron replied: 'I am distressed because you are all doomed to die. Early in the morning some fishermen passed this way and I heard them saying that tomorrow at sunrise they would bring their nets here and catch all the fish in the lake. That's why I am crying, I feel sincerely sorry for you.'

The frightened fish shoaled and discussed the problem. One of them said: 'We must ask the heron to help us. He can save us, because he knows how to fly.' So they swam up to the heron and said: 'If we perish you will perish too, for if the fishermen catch us all there will be nothing left for you to feed on. We have a suggestion: take us in your beak, one by one, and carry us to some other lake where we will be safe. We can all settle there, and you can go on catching and eating us as you have always done. It will be for the good of all of us.'

The sly heron agreed. With no effort whatever he picked up one fish after another and, flying a little way off, ate them greedily. But an old whiskered crab, a friend of the fishes, saw this foul play and decided to save the rest of the fish from the greedy heron. The crab crawled up the shore, and pretending to be very frightened, begged: 'Dear heron, please save me too!' The heron thought: 'I've had enough fish for today. It wouldn't be bad to have a bit of juicy crab-meat for a change.' And he picked the crab up in his beak, intending to fly away and eat him. But the crab caught his neck with his pincers, and snipped off his head. And so he saved the fishes' lives...

The jackal came to the end of his story, and added: 'That's why I say that the only way to fight a stronger enemy is by cunning.'

Tales Told by the Wanderer in Kadas

The crows asked: 'What would you advise us to do?'

The jackal replied: 'Wait until the queens and the ladies-in-waiting come to bathe in the Water-lily lake. When they take off their clothes and jewels and leave them on the beach, steal the most precious necklace, and take it to the cobra's lair. The guards will have to get it back and will kill the cobra.'

And that is exactly what happened. When the queens and their ladies-in-waiting were bathing in the Water-lily lake, both the crows flew to the beach and stole the most precious necklace, the one with the most dazzling glitter of precious stones. They carried it away, flying very slowly to make sure the guards could easily follow them. Then they dropped it into the cobra's lair and sat on the tree-top. The guards went for the necklace, and when they saw the cobra they beat it to death with sticks. From then on the crow couple lived in peace and brought up many little crows...

The crow came to the end of the story and added: 'That's why I say that the only way to fight a stronger enemy is by cunning.'

The owl, offended by the crow's words, said indignantly: 'All the birds have agreed to elect me as their king and only you object. It's the majority that decides, there's no doubt about that!'

The crow laughed and said: 'Yes, owl, the majority decides, but very often just by superiority of numbers, not by the truth. That's how the holy man lost his billy-goat.'

'How did that happen?' asked the birds.

The crow began...

'A holy man was begging at a farm and the rich farmer gave him a billy-goat. He put it on his back and went home. On his way he met three rogues, who made up their minds to cheat him of the billy-goat. So they each went their own way, caught up with the holy man, and running along with him in turn, one at a time or two of them or the three of them together, kept on shouting at him: 'Hey, holy man, why are you carrying an unclean pig on your back?'

'You ought to be ashamed of yourself! A holy man touching a pig!'

'What is this? Even holy men are becoming unclean nowadays!'

The holy man was perturbed. He thought: 'Something must be wrong. I was given a billy-goat, but since so many people claim that it is a pig, it must have been changed by evil spirits!'

He took the billy-goat off his back, stood it on the ground, and examined it carefully. 'Oh yes, it is a billy-goat,' he said to himself, 'it has two nice little horns, a long beard, white hair. It certainly is a billy-goat and those men are fools. He put the goat on his back again, and went on.

But the rogues did not give up. They kept on teasing him, shouting at him and mocking him.

'The world must be coming to an end! Holy men now carry pigs on their backs!'

'For shame! For shame! Do you think you'll get to heaven with a pig?'

'Don't touch us, for heaven's sake! Anyone who carries a pig is a pig himself!'

The wretched holy man thought: 'Am I out of my senses? Perhaps it's an evil omen! There are many strange things in this world. It could be that a demon has turned into a pig and at the same time bewitched my senses.'

He threw the goat on the ground and ran home to make himself clean in a bath. The rogues snatched the billy-goat, cooked it, and had a good meal...

That was the end of the crow's story. The offended owl flew away. The birds then agreed to discuss the matter of the election of their king some other time, as there was no need to hurry.

And ever since, the crows and the owls have disliked each other.

The story of the holy man and his billy-goat amused everyone, young and old. The wandering story-teller picked up his iktar, played a little tune and sang:

'Though the story seems a lie
Truth is hidden from the eye,
What's a lie and what is true?
Make a guess, it's up to you.'

And he began another story.

Mango and the Four Brothers

In the middle of the jungle stood an old tree. Every spring it flowered with thousands of blossoms giving the forest-bees a rich feast. But one springtime only a single bud appeared on it. It was unusually large, all white except for the edges of the outer petals, which were turning pink.

'Why has the old tree only one single bud this year?' the wild animals asked each other. 'And why is the bud so big?'

But none of them knew the answer. The only one who did know it was the vulture, who was a hundred years old. He said: 'The secret of the jungle is hidden in that bud. It will flower one day at midnight, in thunder and lightning. Then you will see for yourselves.'

But the monkeys and the jackals said they were afraid of the storm. The parrots said that at midnight they would be fast asleep and therefore could not see anything. The cobra said he was not interested in that kind of thing. The ants said they were far too busy. The butterflies said that during a thunderstorm the rain would wash the pollen off their wings and they would not be able to fly.

But the owl, the spider, the bears and the baby-bears, the wolves, the tigers, and the elephants all said they would like to see it with their own eyes. And all the surrounding trees, bushes, herbs and grasses agreed that when the storm came at midnight, they would watch the mysterious bud to see the secret of the jungle.

And then at midnight a terrible storm began. Lightning flashed all over the skies, heavy thunder made the earth tremble. The old tree lowered the bough with the bud to the ground, the bud burst open, and a little boy slid out of it.

'He is naked and will catch a cold,' cried a baby-bear. 'Why hasn't he got a fur coat like me?'

'Or why hasn't he got feathers like me?' asked the owl.

'Why hasn't he got leaves like us?' wondered the trees.

The leader of the elephant herd swung his trunk and said: 'We must help him, or he will perish in the jungle.'

And so the grasses wove a bed for him, the trees made a roof of their leaves over it, the bears and the tigers gave him some of their hair, the spider wove a coat for him, the fig-tree gave him sweet figs and the elephants carried him to the well whenever he was thirsty. They all took good care of him.

'It is our child,' they said, 'but we don't know its name.'

The old tree rustled: 'Mango — his name is Mango.'

And Mango grew and gained strength. He was the darling of the whole jungle. The trees, the bushes, and the grasses taught him to know all the berries, those he could eat and those which were poisonous. The bears and the tigers showed him where to find healing herbs and how to use them. The monkeys taught him to climb trees. The giant turtle, who lived in the river, taught him to swim. They all loved him and brought him up as well as they could.

When he had grown to be a strong, slim young man, he asked his old tree: 'Are there any other creatures like me anywhere? Here in the jungle everyone is my friend, but they all have brothers and sisters, only I am alone and have no kin.'

'Why do you ask, Mango?'

'I would like to meet someone who is like me,' answered Mango.

'Then climb to my top branch and look in the direction of the setting sun.'

Mango climbed up the old tree, and saw a high wooded hill. 'On top of that hill,' said the old tree, 'grows my brother. Go and ask him where the Four Brothers are. He will tell you where to go.'

Mango thanked the old tree, said goodbye to it and to all his friends, and set out for the high hill. On the hill-top the brother of the old tree was in blossom. Mango greeted him and asked where he could find the Four Brothers.

'They are in the valley on the other side of the hill, and are just preparing a stag they killed, for dinner,' replied the old tree's brother.

Mango walked down to the valley, and from a distance could see four sturdy hunters cutting up a stag. When they saw Mango, all four of them walked toward him, smiling.

'Welcome,' they said. 'We are the Four Brothers. Do you want to stay with us? There'll be five of us then.'

'That is why I have come,' replied Mango. 'I lived behind the hill in the jungle. Everyone was my friend, but I had no brothers.'

'Very well! Come and have some stag-meat with us.'

And Mango went, and from then on he had four brothers, and the Four Brothers had a fifth one.

'We would like to roast our meat on a fire, but we don't have one. We would like to get married, but here is no one to marry,' said the eldest brother to Mango one day. 'Not far away from here lives the bad giant, Guh-Guh. There is a fire burning in his hearth all the time, and he has four pretty daughters who would like to get married, but he is so terrible that we are afraid to let him set eyes on us, not to mention asking him for fire and his daughters.'

Mango said he would try to get to the giant's house and bring back at least a burning twig. And he went straight away.

The giant Guh-Guh was lying on a heap of furskins in front of the hearth, snoring. There were whole tree-trunks burning in the hearth, which was large as a cave. Mango crept stealthily towards it, snatched a burning twig, and was about to run away, when a spark landed on the giant's face. He gave a cry of pain, woke up, and rushed after Mango to punish him. Mango managed to get away but he dropped the burning twig, so that they were all without fire again.

The Four Brothers told him it was not worth provoking the bad giant, but Mango said: 'I'll try again. Give me a dry gourd, a straight stick and some stag-gut.'

In two days Mango made a lute out of these things, and played it. The brothers liked the music, but they still had no idea what Mango meant to do

The next morning Mango took the lute and went to visit the giant Guh-Guh again. He crept quietly to the house, climbed a big tree growing next to the gate and waited for the giant to take his afternoon nap on the furskins in front of the fire-place. When the giant fell asleep, Mango began to play softly.

The giant Guh-Guh thought at first that he was dreaming. Then he opened one eye, and walked out of the house. The music sounded almost sad, but after a while Mango began to play faster and more gaily, until the giant started dancing round the yard.

His wife looked out of the window, shouting at him: 'What on earth are you doing, you old fool! Hopping around like a clown! You'd do much better looking for husbands for our girls!' Giants' wives have a ready tongue and always have their say.

But Guh-Guh went on dancing, and when his wife and four daughters came out of the house they started to dance too.

Then Mango climbed down the tree, and Guh-Guh said to him: 'You are a one! What can I give you for making me so cheerful?'

Mango said: 'If you want to, you can give me fire and your four daughters for my four brothers.'

'I'll be glad to do that,' said Guh-Guh happily. 'There's plenty of fire here, and having all these women in the house was just too much for me anyway.'

And so Mango brought back fire and wives for his brothers. But being the cleverest of them all, he himself never married.

With this, Jagannath concluded his story-telling in Kadas. He slept in the house of a member of the elders' council, and early in the morning he continued his journey. He was heading for Vada. The stony and dusty plains ended outside Kadas, and Jagannath entered the jungle. Grey apes with long black arms and long tails were romping among the tree-tops. It was damp and dim. Animals and birds could be heard but not seen in the maze of tangled branches, lianas, trunks, stems, bushes, shrubs, grass and flowers. The path, wide enough at first, where it had been beaten by buffalo carts and washed by last year's rains, gradually became narrow and overgrown. At noon-time Jagannath had a light meal, and then he walked on. When it was beginning to get dark, he found a nice spreading fig-tree with wide, flat branches. He climbed one of them, and leaning against the tree-trunk settled down to sleep. So he spent the night, and in the morning continued on his way. He walked almost the whole day, until just outside Vada he crossed a light bridge built of wood and bamboo canes, and at last he was in Vada.

Being thirsty, Jagannath stopped in a small hut at the beginning of the village, and bought some sugar-cane syrup. The two boys who were selling it recognised him at once: 'Jagannath is here! Jagannath has come!' they shouted excitedly. And soon all of Vada knew that the wandering story-teller had arrived. After Jagannath had bathed and eaten a little, everyone came, and Jagannath began a story.

Jasu's Adventures in Cambodia

Once upon a time, in the country of Gond, there was a king who had eight sons. The youngest one was Jasu, and he was a most handsome, clever and skilful prince. Because of this his brothers were not fond of him, but the old king loved him. Jasu was his favourite son.

One day the king of Gond summoned his counsellors and said to them: 'I see that I am getting older and weaker every day. When I die and go to the realm of the god of Death, I want Jasu to sit on the throne, because of all my sons only he will be fit to govern our country. Thus I have decreed, and my decision is irreversible.'

The counsellors bowed, and promised to bear in mind the king's wish and to act in accordance with it. The news soon spread all over the royal court. Most of the courtiers were not even surprised, because the whole country knew the princes' dispositions and ways; but Jasu's brothers were very unpleasantly surprised and became very angry.

'Our father is the king, true, but he must be getting feeble-minded with old age, if he has chosen that milksop Jasu as his heir to the throne,' said the oldest prince. 'We must do something about it!' The other brothers also showed their discontent by shouting loudly, and one of them suggested: 'Let's go down to the bank of the river Mahanadi and wrestle. Jasu will want to join us, and during the fight we'll throw him in the river, where the alligators will devour him!'

'That is an excellent idea,' agreed all the brothers, and they went to the river Mahanadi at once.

Jasu was sitting in the palace at the feet of his father, the king, talking to him. When he heard his brothers' boisterous voices, he said: 'My brothers are probably learning to wrestle on the river bank. Allow me to go and join them.'

'You had better not go there, Jasu,' replied the king. 'Your brothers don't like you; in fact, they hate you. They might want to hurt you.'

'How do you know, father?' wondered Jasu.

'I can see it in their eyes. They can't hide their hatred for you any more than a dog can hide its tail.'

But Jasu said: 'I'm sure they won't hurt me. After all, I am their own brother.' And so the king unwillingly gave his consent.

As soon as the brothers saw Jasu approaching them they shouted at him: 'Come and wrestle with us. Come on, don't be afraid — we know you are the youngest and the weakest of us. We'll spare you.'

These remarks made Jasu indignant and he rushed headlong into the fight. He wrestled with each of the brothers in turn, and when he had tired, the eldest brother cried: 'Now!' And all of them pounced upon Jasu like a swarm of bumble-bees on a single water-lily.

His father's words came to Jasu's mind and he knew at once what they meant to do. Summoning all his strength, he broke loose from their hold and threw them one after another in the air. They fell on the sandy shore of the river Mahanadi, their bones cracking. Jasu who, although he was the youngest, was nevertheless the strongest and most skilful, laughed at them and left them lying there humiliated and angry.

The eldest brother said to the others, gritting his teeth: 'We can't go on like this. It's a terrible disgrace! If we can't get rid of Jasu, let's sail to foreign lands in the east.' The rest of them agreed, and so the seven brothers prepared for a long journey. The king did not try to restrain them, because he knew if they fared well abroad they would stay there, if not, they would return home.

The king's grandmother, an old sorceress, sent for Jasu and said to him: 'My dear Jasu, your brothers are going to sail to foreign lands in the east. Go with them, for there in the land of Cambodia, lives Princess Sukrita, whom fate has ordained to be your wife. But it will not be an easy task to win her. That is why I will give you something to take along.' And she gave him a short bamboo stick, which was sealed at both ends.

'There are three things inside this bamboo case, all of which will be of good use to you,' explained the old sorceress to her great-grandson. 'One is a betel leaf; just touch it with your lips, and you will stop feeling hungry or thirsty. The second is a little magic figure made of wood, which I have endowed with the three magic powers of the earth, the air, and the waters. Whenever you are in need of advice or help, take the figure out of the case and say:

'Hunu, hear me,
Hunu, look at me,
Hunu, help me!

And then take whatever advice Hunu gives you. The third is a large ruby which will protect you from all bad creatures that run, fly or swim; just hold it firmly in your hand, and any animal threatening you will turn to a heap of ashes.'

Jasu sincerely thanked his great-grandmother for her advice and the gift, but she added: 'When I was young, which is very long ago, I was taught by the old wizard Jamrup, who has for centuries, or perhaps for thousands of years, lived at the well of the Water of Life, in the deepest abyss of the deepest valley over the great ocean. I have put all the best things he has taught me into this bamboo case, because I want to help you, and because I know that you will need them. My brother Nand and my sister Nanda are still serving as Jamrup's assistants. If you ever get there, and I think it is quite probable, give them my regards.'

Jasu bowed his head to his great-grandmother's feet in respect and gratitude, bade her farewell, and placing the bamboo case in a fold of his gown, went to join his brothers. 'My elder brothers,' he said, 'I see you are rigging a boat, setting sails, fixing oars and storing food and drinking-water. I see you are going to sail to foreign lands in the east. Take me with you, dear brothers!'

The eldest one retorted: 'Never! You're the very reason why we are leaving home for unknown lands, where we don't know what might befall us.'

'Although I am the youngest,' insisted Jasu, 'I am sure I would be a help, not a burden. The more of us there are in foreign lands, the better for us.'

The other brothers winked secretly at the eldest who, realising that it would be easier to get rid of Jasu abroad, said: 'All right, we'll take you with us. But I am the leader, and you will obey me like the rest.' And Jasu promised he would.

Then all the brothers took leave of the king, and sailed off on the waves of the great river Mahanadi, eastward, towards the boundless ocean. The journey was arduous. Enormous waves tossed the boat about, sharks and alligators showed their sharp teeth. The largest of them tried to turn the boat over, beating it with their huge tails. Tigers and leopards peered at them from shrubs on the shore, brightly coloured poisonous snakes crawled in the grass and through the bushes. Twice the moon filled with sweet nectar, and twice the gods drank it before the brothers arrived in their boat at the place where the great river Mahanadi flows into the ocean.

There they landed on the shore, tied up the boat, and asked each other: 'What now? Shall we stay here, or shall we walk along the coast? But which way? Towards noon, or midnight? Wouldn't it be better to go inland? Or perhaps we should build huts here, and live on what the sea and the woods supply us with?'

But now Jasu spoke: 'Would the hardships we endured while we were sailing the river Mahanadi be worth it, if we were to stay here on the barren shore, living on fish, mussels and berries? I thought you had more courage, brothers. Untie the boat, set sail and use the oars! We'll sail on eastward! Let's cross the ocean and see what's in store for us there.'

Embarrassed, the brothers looked at each other, not knowing what to say.

'If you are afraid, you can stay here or go wherever you like,' said Jasu resolutely. 'But I am putting to sea. If you wish, you can come with me. I won't force you though.'

The brothers felt ashamed for having lost heart, and at last the eldest said hesitatingly: 'We would also like to continue eastward. Indeed, we have almost decided to continue across the ocean. But we are afraid' — now his regained pride was speaking — 'that you will be a burden to us. After all, you are the youngest and cannot endure as much as we can.'

Jasu answered with a laugh: 'You needn't be afraid of that, brothers! I can endure at least as much as you. And I am willing to submit to the leadership of our eldest brother, and to obey him in every way. I promise you that.'

And so they all sailed across the sea and the ocean, heading east. They suffered greater hardships than those they had experienced on the river Mahanadi. The waves were as tall as their father's royal palace, sharks and monsters of all kinds swarmed around them below the surface, emerging to fix their unmoving eyes on the brothers, as if they were waiting for an opportunity to devour them. There was a fresh wind blowing from the mainland, the sails swelled, and the brothers did not spare their arms, pulling the oars so fast that the boat skimmed across the water like an arrow. Soon the land-line disappeared from the horizon, and there was only the wide fathomless ocean surrounding them.

They had been sailing for many days, feeding on fish and quenching their thirst with the morning dew which had fallen on the sides of the boat. Jasu was the most fortunate of them. Every evening when darkness came and his brothers lay down to rest, leaving the boat to float with the current and the wind, he took the green betel leaf out of the bamboo case, put it to his lips — and his hunger and thirst were stilled immediately.

But his brothers were weaker every day, their bodies skinny, looking like dry branches torn off the spreading fig-tree by a hail storm. They were not strong enough to pull the oars any more, and were fainting from weariness. Jasu then said to himself: 'I know they hate me, but after all, they are my brothers. I can't let them die of hunger and thirst.'

He took the green betel leaf out of the bamboo case, and while they were sleeping, he put it to the lips of each of his exhausted brothers. They were all rid of hunger and thirst, and strength flowed back into their tired muscles. Feeling refreshed, they took hold of the oars thinking: 'How strange! Suddenly we don't feel hungry or thirsty and we're as fresh and strong as when we set sail! We must be approaching a fertile land, full of juicy fruit, large rice and heavy corn, since even the breeze blowing from the coast has blown away our fatigue and weariness.'

Only Jasu knew the truth, and he did not tell them.

The next day they met a small fishing-boat. The eldest brother called to the fisherman: 'Hail! Which way lies the nearest coast and what is the name of the country?'

'Hail, strangers,' replied the fisherman. 'Our country lies in the course of your bow, and it is called Cambodia. If you sail on at the same speed, you will see the coastline tomorrow before sunrise.'

The brothers thanked him, and pulled at the oars with vigour. They had never heard of a country called Cambodia. But Jasu remembered what his great-grandmother had told him, and he knew that this country was ruled by Princess Sukrita.

When night had fallen and his brothers were asleep, Jasu took the magic figure out of the bamboo case, and whispered:

'Hunu, hear me,

Hunu, look at me,

Hunu, help me!'

The figure quivered slightly, opened its eyes, and in a voice as thin as the humming of a mosquito, it said: 'What do you wish, master?'

'Tell me,' demanded Jasu, 'about Cambodia, and its ruler, Princess Sukrita.'

'Cambodia is a beautiful, rich country. Its woods are full of wild animals and game, its waters swarm with fish and other living things, its mountains abound with precious stones and metals. Its fields yield rice and other crops in unusually great quantities. But no stranger has ever seen Princess Sukrita, for everyone has met with death as soon as he landed on the coast. The sandy shore of Cambodia is strewn with the bones of those who ventured to court the princess, and the bones are bleached by salt water and the parching sun.' So spoke Hunu.

Jasu asked: 'And is Princess Sukrita pretty?'

'She is in the bloom of her youth,' was the soft reply. 'And words cannot describe her beauty. She is as delicate as a banana-blossom, stars twinkle in her eyes, and her smile makes men faint in ecstasy.'

'How can I come to see her?' continued Jasu.

'You will never set eyes on her unless you outwit and overcome her guardian, the huge tiger Vyaghra, whose eyes are so sharp, nose so sensitive, ears so perceptive that he can see, sense and hear anyone who approaches the coast of Cambodia,' said Hunu softly. 'During the day he sleeps in a great cavern close to the royal palace, during the night he paces the shore and tears to pieces anyone he falls upon as easily as naughty boys tear the wings off butterflies. He is as large as an elephant, and when he roars it sounds like the thunder the god Indra lets loose in his anger. And you will also have to fight the princess's four older brothers, who can turn into bald buzzards.'

Then Hunu became silent and closed his eyes. Jasu put him back in the bamboo case and dreamed of the lovely Princess Sukrita.

Before sunrise the boat approached the Cambodian coast. The huge tiger Vyaghra roared and the princess's four brothers turned into bald buzzards and flew to the shore like a shot. They saw the boat with Jasu and his brothers, and returning to Princess Sukrita they said: 'A boat with eight men on board is approaching our coast. What do you want us to do now?'

'Ask those strangers,' said Princess Sukrita, 'whether they come with good or bad intentions. If their intentions be good, tell them to sail away in peace immediately. If their intentions be bad, they will die!'

The bald buzzards promptly returned to the shore, and addressed the brothers who had meanwhile descended on shore: 'Why have you landed here, strangers? Are your intentions good or bad?'

Jasu knew at once that these were Princess Sukrita's brothers, and so he said to his own brothers: 'Be kind to them and all will end well!'

But his eldest brother rebuked him roughly: 'You keep your mouth shut! You're the youngest, and think yourself the cleverest of all of us! Hold your tongue and let me do the talking!' And turning to the bald buzzards he retorted rudely: 'It's none of your business, you sea-robbers! We landed here because we felt like it, and we'll do whatever we want!' And he threw a stone at them.

The birds croaked angrily, soared up into the skies, and vanished. They told the princess: 'Sister, these strangers have come with bad intentions and have insulted us badly!'

At that Princess Sukrita took her long thunderbolt-flinging lance and ran to the shore to punish the insolent strangers.

Jasu took out the magic figure, and after saying the magic formula, when it opened its eyes, he asked: 'Now we are in danger of our lives. What shall I do?'

Hunu replied: 'Dive in the water straight away and hide below the surface, because the angry Princess Sukrita will kill all your brothers and destroy your boat. But she will not see you and you will be saved.'

Jasu did so at once — and at the same time Princess Sukrita appeared   a beautiful outraged maiden, the sovereign of Cambodia with the terrible lance in her hand, flinging deadly thunderbolts. She killed all of Jasu's brothers and smashed the boat to pieces with it. Then she returned to her palace and said to her brothers: 'Vyaghra has kept watch well, even though he sleeps in his cavern, and you too have watched well. But remain watchful, for strangers seldom bring any good!'

Jasu, who from the depth had not been able to take a single look at the princess, emerged from the waves all out of breath and stepped ashore. The terrible tiger Vyaghra, though he was sleeping, roared again.

Princess Sukrita exclaimed in surprise: 'It seems I have not killed all the strangers. One of them must have hidden under the water! Or is Vyaghra dreaming and roaring in his sleep?' She then asked her four brothers to fly to the shore after all, and take a look if any stranger happened to be there.

Jasu heard Vyaghra's terrible roar and promptly asked Hunu, the magic figure made of wood, what he should do now.

'Your ruby will not help you here, because it has power over animals that run, fly or swim, but not over human beings, even though they are changed into buzzards. And then, if you killed the princess's brothers, she would never forgive you, and never could love you,' said Hunu. 'Here you must resort to guile. I will tell you their names. If you call them by their own names, they will be so overwhelmed that they will not dare to hurt you. Listen carefully and remember that the names of Sukrita's brothers are Dam, Daman, Damanan, Damananan. Repeat the names after me because if you forget a single one of them the result will be very bad for you.'

'Dam, Daman, Damanan, Damananan,' repeated Jasu without

a mistake, and Hunu closed his eyes and became a motionless wooden figure again.

Hardly had Jasu put Hunu back in the bamboo case than the swift wings of four buzzards whizzed through the air. With cruel yellow eyes and menacing beaks they bore down on Jasu, wanting to peck out his eyes and smash his skull. Jasu shuddered, but overcame his fear and cried: 'Hail, friends! I salute you, Dam, and you also, Daman, Damanan and Damananan! I do not come with bad intentions!' And he held out his hands to show that he had no weapon.

The buzzards slowed their flight and began to circle around Jasu. The oldest of them said in a human voice: 'Who are you, stranger, and how is it that you know our names, which, besides ourselves, are known only to our sister, the princess and sovereign of Cambodia? Where do you come from and what do you seek here?'

'I am Jasu and have come by boat with my brothers from our father's kingdom, which lies on the banks of the river Mahanadi far in the west. Fate has ordained your sister Sukrita to become my wife. That is why I am here,' replied Jasu truthfully.

The buzzards were immensely surprised and said to each other: 'What luck it is we did not hurt him. He must be a very powerful man and must practise magic of all sorts, for not only does he know our names but also the name of our sister. He wouldn't be a bad husband for her. She's not likely to find a better one. And if he has really been ordained for her by fate, then we cannot do anything about it anyway. Let's turn into human beings again, and talk it over with him.'

And they did as they had said. Three times they turned around in the air, and suddenly, standing in front of Jasu there were four strong young men, all looking alike, like four fruits of the same tree.

'We apologize to you, Jasu,' said the eldest, 'for a slightly rough welcome. You see, we have had bad experience with strangers, whatever their origin. But you seem to be good and with no bad intentions. I am sure you would be a most suitable husband for our sister but I must openly say that I fear there will be certain difficulties. For our sister is quite wilful and does not like to do anything she has not decided for herself, like a true princess. You can be assured of our friendship and support, but in dealing with our sister be as wary as a snake and as mistrustful as a raven, until you are certain that she really loves you.'

Jasu thanked the four brothers, and they all agreed that when the brothers told Sukrita that they had found a suitable husband for her, who had been ordained for her by fate, Jasu would come to the castle and be introduced to the princess. Then the brothers turned into buzzards again and flew to the castle.

Jasu took Hunu out of the bamboo case and asked: 'What shall I do now? I don't want to spoil things. Help me, Hunu!'

'So far you have done very well, indeed, excellently. But now you must be careful,' said Hunu in his soft voice. 'Princess Sukrita will not submit to her brothers' wishes readily, and she is sure to set her tiger Vyaghra against you. But you will easily turn him to ashes with your ruby. A far more difficult task will be to overcome her wilfulness. But that we will leave for a later time.' And he closed his eyes and became stiff.

In the meantime the four brothers came to the castle and turned into human beings. They went to their sister at once and told her how they had met a stranger on the shore whose name was Jasu, and who had come with his brothers by boat from a distant country in the west. The eldest brother then said: 'And since this man appeals to us and has great magic power, we have chosen him to become your husband. It is high time you married, dear sister, and this man has been ordained for you by fate. In a little while he will come to the palace to pay you his respects. What do you say to this?'

Princess Sukrita frowned and exclaimed indignantly: 'You have dared to decide without consulting me? You want to force me to marry a man I don't even know? We shall see about that!'

The brothers did not utter a single word, they just looked at each other uneasily. But the princess realised she would find it easier to get rid of the unknown suitor by guile, and so she smiled at them and said sweetly: 'When I think of it, you are probably right, dear brothers. If he really is the man you say, I will be glad to marry him. Call the servants and order them to prepare a fine betrothal banquet!'

The brothers were pleased and did as Sukrita wanted. But the princess hurried to the cavern where the terrible tiger Vyaghra was sleeping at this time of the day. Vyaghra was panting heavily and snoring, and the princess shook him saying: 'Oh my tiger, my only true guardian! Wake up and save me! Even my brothers want to make me marry; now you are the only one I can rely on!' But the tiger slept on and on. Sukrita bent down, picked up a sharp stone and with all her strength she threw it straight at the tiger's nose. Vyaghra roared, woke up and the princess quickly commanded: 'Run to the shore as fast as you can! There is a stranger there. Tear him to pieces and save me!'

The tiger set off for the shore in long leaps. His eyes flashed lightning, his tail swung to and fro. The princess ran out of the cavern and shouted: 'Tear him to pieces! Kill him! Destroy him!'

When Jasu saw the tiger rushing at him, he quickly took the magic ruby from the bamboo case and clasped it in his hand — and the terrible tiger roared for the last time and turned into a heap of ashes.

Then Jasu went to the castle. Princess Sukrita stood in the gateway waiting for her guardian tiger to return, but instead she saw Jasu walking towards her. Not only had he not been torn to pieces, there was not a single scratch on his body. She suppressed her anger and ill-humour and went to meet him. In a kind voice she invited him to the palace where a splendid banquet was ready. But in her mind she was planning mischief. When no one was looking she poured the contents of a phial of poison in the drink which was prepared for Jasu on the table. And she looked forward to having her own way.

Jasu sat down in his place, Princess Sukrita seated herself next to him, and her brothers sat on both sides of them. Then Sukrita took her cup: 'Welcome, Jasu, my prince from the distant western country! Let's drink a toast!' And she lifted her cup. Jasu remembered Hunu's last words and said: 'Hail, princess, ordained to me by fate. I will gladly drink a toast with you, but first tell me truthfully if perchance there is poison in my cup. Whatever your answer be, I shall drink it, because if you are the one to wish me dead, then life has no meaning for me, even if I should stay alive. But I would like to know the truth first.'

'You can drink the toast with me, my prince. There is no poison in your cup,' said Sukrita. But she was lying.

Jasu lifted his cup to his lips, but at that moment Princess Sukrita knocked it out of his hand, and apologising for being so clumsy she handed him a red pomegranate: 'You had better have some fruit, my dear Jasu! Now I see that you really are the man fate has ordained to be my husband.' She embraced him gently and kissed him. At last Jasu was certain that Princess Sukrita really loved him. Now he had nothing to fear. 'My brothers were right, you are the right man for me,' added Princess Sukrita, smiling sweetly at Jasu.

Soon a wedding as glorious as befits princes and princesses took place at the palace. For a long time afterwards the whole country talked about it, because no one had ever seen anything as glorious and splendid anywhere.

And so Jasu won Princess Sukrita, who had been ordained to him by fate, and became the king of Cambodia.

But he was very sad because his brothers were dead. Once on a warm spring night he had a dream. He saw his seven brothers coming to him from the shore. They bowed to him and clasped their hands before their brows in greeting. Then they sat down at his feet and the eldest said: 'Dear brother, our king, we have wronged you greatly. Our minds were dimmed with pride and envy and that was our undoing. We have come to beg your forgiveness, for our souls cannot find peace otherwise. Forgive us, brother!'

At that moment Jasu woke up. He missed his brothers more and more, and his grief was deeper every day. Then he remembered what his great-grandmother had told him before his departure, when she had given him the three magic gifts in the bamboo case, about the wizard Jamrup who lived at the well of the Water of Life. And it occurred to him that he might bring his brothers back to life with it.

He immediately took the magic figure in his hand and said:

'Hunu, hear me,

Hunu, look at me,

Hunu, help me!'

The figure quivered, opened its eyes, and in a voice as thin as the humming of a mosquito, said: 'What do you wish, master?'

'Tell me,' demanded Jasu, 'where is the well of the Water of Life, the place where the wizard Jamrup lives?'

'It is very far from here,' answered Hunu. 'The Water of Life springs from the deepest abyss of the deepest valley beyond four jungles, six rivers and eight mountains in the direction of midnight. There the wizard Jamrup abides. His body is as withered with age as a tree-trunk struck by a thunderbolt, and is as black as the charcoal the colliers burn in the woods. Each day, in the middle of the night, Jamrup stretches his hands to the well and a coconut-shell cup emerges from it, filled with the Water of Life. Jamrup takes it and never gives a drop to anyone. If you want to obtain the Water of Life and revive your brothers with it, you must fool him. Jamrup has two assistants. Nand is

his guard, and Nanda keeps the fire burning. You will have to fool them too.'

'Nand and Nanda are the brother and sister of my great-grandmother.' said Jasu.

'In that case, since they are your kin, they will help you.' Hunu became silent, closed his eyes, and was motionless.

Jasu could not wait for the morning to come. When the sun rose above the horizon he told his wife, Sukrita, about his dream, and about his decision to go to the deepest abyss in the deepest valley beyond four jungles, six rivers, and eight mountains to take wizard Jamrup's shell with the Water of Life, and revive his brothers. Sukrita began to weep and embracing him she begged Jasu: 'Don't go to that terrible distant place; you will perish there, and I shall die of sorrow. Don't go, don't leave me!'

'Stop crying and sighing, dear Sukrita,' Jasu soothed her gently and stroked her hair. 'It is no use, for I have made up my mind to bring my brothers back to life, and no man changes his decision because of a woman's tears. I will leave at once, for the sooner I go, the sooner I shall return. But please take care of yourself here, because should anything happen to you in the meantime, it would be the end of me.' Then he bade farewell to Sukrita and her four brothers, to whose care he had left her, and went. The only thing he took with him was the bamboo case with the three magic gifts his great-grandmother had given him.

He went on and on in the direction of midnight, and although he was tired he did not stop to rest until he had crossed four jungles, six rivers and eight mountains, stilling his hunger and thirst with the green betel leaf. At last he saw in front of him the deepest valley and in the middle of it the deepest abyss. Standing there was a large, strong old man armed with a magic lance.

The old man aimed the point of his lance at Jasu and said sternly in a voice that sounded like the croaking of a whole flock of vultures: 'Who are you, you audacious young man, and what do you want here?'

'I am Jasu, the son of the king of Gond, the great-grandson of your sister, and you must be Nand. My great-grandmother sends you her regards,' replied Jasu, and he clasped his hands.

'What!' said Nand, surprised. 'If that is the case, since you are my kin, I will have to let you go anywhere you wish, even to the abyss. And

I will be glad to do it for you.' He lowered his lance and continued: 'Evidently you have come for the Water of Life. But whether you succeed in getting it or not, be careful on your way back not to trip over the root of the sacred fig-tree, because wizard Jamrup would hear its leaves rustle and would wake up and punish you by death!'

Jasu thanked Nand and descended into the abyss. When he came to the bottom, he looked around and close to the fire he saw a large, strong old woman standing with an axe in her hand.

The old woman lifted the axe and said sternly in a voice that sounded like the croaking of a whole flock of crows: 'Who are you, you audacious young man, and what do you want here?'

'I am the son of the king of Gond and the great-grandson of your sister, and you must be Nanda. My great-grandmother sends you her regards,' answered Jasu, and he saluted the old woman with his clasped hands.

'What!' said Nanda surprised. 'If that is the case, since you are my kin, I will have to help you with whatever you wish, even to gain the shell filled with the Water of Life. And I will be glad to do it for you.' She put down the axe and continued: 'Be very quiet, for you mustn't awaken wizard Jamrup who is sleeping at the well. Should he wake up, he would punish you by death!'

She embraced Jasu and bade him sit down in front of the hearth. Then she took a handful of cold ashes and blackened her arms with them up to the armpits. Jasu watched the procedure with great interest. Nanda quietly went to the well and because it was just midnight, she held out her hands above the surface. The water rippled and two hands, delicate as the buds of water-lilies, lifted a coconut shell filled with the Water of Life and held it out. Nanda took it and quietly retreated. The wizard slumbered on peacefully.

Nanda gave the shell with the Water of Life to Jasu and whispered: 'Now hurry away before Jamrup wakes up. Farewell, and the best of luck on your way home!'

Happy Jasu thanked Nanda saying: 'You have helped me to save my seven brothers. Now I will be able to bring them back to life. I shall be grateful to you for the rest of my days.' He bowed to her and hurried out of the deepest abyss.

When he was almost at the top of the deepest abyss of the deepest valley, his foot slipped, and Jasu in an effort not to spill the Water of

Life tripped over the root of the sacred fig-tree. Its leaves rustled, wizard Jamrup woke up from his slumber and shouted out of the abyss: 'Hey, Nand, my guard, what's going on there?'

Nand saw that it was Jasu who had tripped over the root and he answered: 'It's nothing, only a wild boar that ran by and tripped over the root.' The wizard believed him and asked no more questions.

Jasu was very glad, and thanked Nand, saying: 'You have helped me to save my seven brothers. Now I will be able to bring them back to life. I shall be grateful to you for the rest of my days.' He bowed to him and hurried away from the deepest valley.

The way which led over eight mountains, six rivers and four jungles passed so quickly now, that before he could realize it, he was back home with Princess Sukrita. She greeted him, overwhelmed with joy at seeing him safe and sound. She laughed, cried, danced and embraced her Jasu, then kissed him and caressed him.

When they had greeted each other to their hearts' content, Jasu went to the shore, where the bleached bones of his seven brothers lay. He sprinkled them all with the Water of Life — and instantly his brothers stood before him alive and well, as he had last seen them before hiding in the sea from the angry Princess Sukrita.

The brothers clasped their hands before their brows and bowed to Jasu. The eldest said: 'Thank you, our youngest brother, for forgiving us the wrong we have done you and for bringing us back to life. Now we know that although you are the youngest of us, you are the most wise and brave.' Jasu sincerely greeted his brothers and then he led them to the palace to introduce them to his wife Sukrita, and her four brothers. Then a great banquet was arranged and there was joy and good will among all.

When the banquet was over they all boarded a large boat and sailed west to the kingdom of Gond. The aged king and his wise old grandmother were happy to see the eight brothers return as friends and to meet Jasu's charming wife and his four brothers-in-law.

The old king of Gond then gave his rule over to Jasu as he had decided long ago, and so Jasu became the ruler of a second kingdom. And always he ruled one year in the kingdom of Gond, the next year in the kingdom of Cambodia. During his absence the kingdoms were ruled in turns by his brothers and his brothers-in-law, together, in unity and peace.

Thousands of stars twinkled in the dark sky, and bats silently glided through the air. The wandering story-teller picked up his iktar and played a little tune. Then he sang:

'Though the story seems a lie
Truth is hidden from the eye.
What's a lie, and what is true?
Make a guess, it's up to you.'

And he began another story.

Of the Good Elephant

In the Himalayan virgin forests there once lived a large white elephant with beautiful long tusks. He was a wise elephant who had experienced many things, both good and bad, but for all this he remained good-natured and kind. The white elephant knew that evil breeds only evil, and so he was friendly and kind to all living creatures. All the animals were fond of him, and whenever any of them were in need of advice they would ask the white elephant, and things would always turn out well.

At one time he had been the leader of all Himalayan elephants, but when the herd became dominated by envy, malice and wickedness, he left to lead a solitary life of meditation and contemplation, helping anyone who needed advice or support. For this reason he was called the Kind Elephant King.

It happened one day that a man got lost in the Himalayan forest.

He could not find his way in the intricate dense maze of trees, bushes, herbs and grasses and in his confusion he ran the one way and the other, coming back and running in circles, wringing his hands, lamenting and calling for help. But there were no other men for a long way.

The white elephant heard his lamentations and decided to help him. He rushed towards him through the bushes, but the man was frightened by the sight of him and ran away. The white elephant stopped. Seeing this the man stopped too. But when the white elephant started towards him again, the man took to flight. And so the white elephant stopped again, and the man thought: 'This white elephant always stops when he sees me running away from him. He probably does not mean to hurt me, because if he wanted, he could have caught up with me long ago. I'll wait for him.' And he stopped running.

The good elephant came up to the man and asked him: 'Why are you shouting and complaining?'

The man answered: 'I have lost my way in this forest and I don't know how to get out. I'm afraid I will perish here.'

'Don't worry,' said the white elephant kindly, 'I will take you to a path which will lead you back to human beings.' He carefully put his trunk round the man's waist, lifted him on his back, and went. But the man was cunning and malicious. Thinking: 'I will have to tell all my friends and neighbours about this,' he looked around curiously in order to remember all the mountains, hills, brooks, rivers and large trees they were passing as the elephant carried him on his back to the path that would lead him out of the forest to human beings.

When they arrived there, the elephant put the man on the ground and said: 'Well, this is your path. It will lead you to Benares. Go, and peace be with you, but I beg you one thing. Don't tell anyone what happened to you and how I helped you, not even if people should ask.' Then he said goodbye and returned to the jungle.

The ungrateful man returned to Benares and went straight to the artisans who made all sorts of useful and decorative things from ivory, and asked them: 'How much would you give me for the large tusks of a live elephant?'

'What a question!' said the eldest artisan. 'The tusks of a live elephant are much more valuable than those of a dead one. Bring them here, and you'll see that you'll get paid very well.'

'I'l bring them to you,' said the wicked man. He took a saw and went back to the Himalayan forest, where the white elephant, the Kind Elephant King, lived. When the white elephant saw the man coming he asked: 'Why have you come back? What brings you here?'

'I have been driven here by need, white elephant,' said the scoundrel. 'I have nothing to eat. Give me one of your tusks. I will sell it in Benares, and then I will be able to buy food.'

The white elephant was at first surprised by his audacious request, but then he said: 'Very well, I shall give you one of my tusks, if you have something to cut it off with.'

'I brought my saw with me,' said the man greedily.

And so the white elephant lay down and let him cut off one of his tusks. But the man said: 'Dear elephant, let me cut off the other one too. You know that tusks go in pairs, and therefore, should be together. You'll save me the trouble of coming back again when I've spent all the money I'll get for the first one.'

This time the man's impudence amazed the elephant, but in the end he allowed him to cut off the other tusk too. Then he said mildly: 'Don't imagine that I'm not fond of my tusks, or that I will not miss them. But if you think ivory tusks will benefit you, take them and sell them.'

The ungrateful fellow grabbed the tusks and left without a word of thanks. He sold them to the artisans for a good price and within a short time had spent all the money. So he went back to the Himalayan forest, and without much ado said to the white elephant: 'Look, I have sold your tusks and the money is gone. I'm poor again and have nothing to eat. Give me the stumps of your tusks for me to sell.'

The kind white elephant consented, because he said to himself that once he had given his tusks, he might as well give him the stumps. The man cut them off, and left. But he soon spent all the money he got for them again, and so he went to the Himalayan forest for the third time.

Without hesitation he told the white elephant: 'You have given me your tusks and their stumps, give me their roots as well, so that I can sell them.'

The kind white elephant concluded that roots are a part of the tusks and therefore should go with them, and he lay down on his side to allow the man to take them. The man mounted the white elephant's head, and kicked him in the place where the beautiful long tusks had grown so long, until he pushed both the roots out. He picked them up and without saying a single word to the elephant he went his way, looking forward to selling the roots with profit to the artisans.

The white elephant, overwhelmed by the man's ruthlessness, watched him walking away, and felt sad at heart. He thought: 'Nevertheless, I have done well to give him everything he wanted. Because every deed bears in itself inevitable results, every cause has consequence, and everyone shall taste the fruit of his own deeds.'

Then Mother-Earth, who can bear the weight of all the mountains and seas; who can bear the swarming and the rushing about of all living creatures; who can even bear the terrible storms, gales and floods, could not bear the heavy weight of the scoundrel's wickedness, greed and ingratitude, and cracking under his feet, swallowed his unworthy body, burying it in her glowing entrails.

The peasants listened spellbound. The wandering story-teller picked up his iktar, played a little tune and then he sang:
'Though the story seems a lie
Truth is hidden from the eye.
What's a lie and what is true?
Make a guess, it's up to you.'
And he began another story.

The Four Treasures

In one town there lived four young men, all very good friends. But they were very poor and often complained of their ill fortune: 'Alas! Alas! What a miserable life we lead! People who have no money, have no respect. Everyone despises them. It's better to be dead than to have no money!'

Once when they were considering what to do or undertake to become wealthier, one of them said: 'I know of a holy man who practises magic of all kinds. Let's go and see him, he's sure to give us some useful advice.'

The next day, early in the morning they left town and travelled over mountains, through the jungle and the desert, and then again through the jungle and over the mountains, until they came to the charming country of Avanti. They reached the pure river Sipra and bathed in its sacred waters. Then they entered a little temple of Shiva, and performed an offering.

In front of the temple they met a holy man. It was the one they had talked of, the holy man who dealt with mystery and magic. They saluted him very respectfully, and he took them to his hermitage.

There he asked them: 'Where are you from? Where are you going? What do you want to do?'

The friends answered: 'We are four friends, and we are so poor that we don't even have anything to eat. We have come to you, oh holy man, for you know all kinds of magic, and we have come to seek your advice. We are ready to try anything, nothing can frighten us. Please be so kind as to tell us what to do!'

The holy man nodded, and said: 'It depends on what you want to

140)

achieve. If you have will-power and determination you can achieve anything you wish. You don't need a holy man's advice for that.'

In a single voice the friends said: 'We have will-power and do not lack determination. We want to gain wealth. That's why we have come to you.'

'Very well,' said the holy man. 'If you are determined to gain wealth, I will help you. Take these four magic balls of thread and go further north to the Himalayan range. Wherever a ball falls from the hands of one of you, there you shall find a treasure buried in the ground.'

The four friends thanked him sincerely for the four thread balls and for his advice, and bade him farewell. But the holy man remarked: 'Take care not to become blinded in your pursuit of wealth! Keep your common-sense!'

And so the four friends set forth to the Himalayas. They had travelled for many days when at last they saw the snow-capped peaks of the Himalayas. And at that very moment one of them dropped his ball of thread.

'The treasure!' he exclaimed. 'The ball has fallen out of my hands, so there must be a treasure here!' and he began to dig there.

After a while he dug up a large pot full of copper coins. Feeling very happy, he said to his friends: 'Let's share them, and we can return home.'

The other three laughed at him: 'Nothing of the kind! Copper coins are almost worthless! Who would want to drag a load like that! Is that what you call wealth? We are going on.'

'As you wish, I'll go back home alone with my treasure.'

And the three friends continued in their journey. A little later the second one dropped his thread ball. He said happily: 'Look, here is my treasure!' and he dug, until he dug up a large pot full of silver coins.

'Let's share them, and return home,' he said to the other two.

'You fool!' they retorted. 'Now we are sure to find gold coins! We don't mean to go back empty-handed.'

And the two of them went on. When one of them dropped his thread ball he began to dig in that place, and he found a pot full of gold coins.

'We were right, after all! The holy man gave us good advice. Now we can share the gold coins, and go home,' he said to his friend.

But the friend rejoined: 'Nonsense! First we found copper coins, then silver coins and now you have found gold coins. I am sure to find pearls and precious stones. I'll go on, you can return home by yourself.'

And the fourth young man went on and on. He suffered hunger and thirst, but the vision of his oncoming wealth gave him strength. He came to a hill, and on top of it saw a man standing, with a large revolving wheel on his head. His face was blood-stained and distorted by pain. Going up to him the young man said: 'Why are you standing here with the wheel turning on your head? It must be torture for you!'

No sooner had he spoken, than the wheel landed on his head and merrily went on spinning. The last of the four friends cried: 'What is this? It hurts me! How am I to get rid of this wheel?'

The strange man answered: 'You'll get rid of it the same way as I did, when someone comes here with a magic ball of thread, in search of pearls and precious stones, and asks you why you are standing here with the revolving wheel on your head.'

'But it's terribly painful!'

'You'll have to bear that, for you have no other choice,' was the stranger's reply. 'If you stand here as long as I had to before you came, you'll realize that knowledge without common-sense leads to destruction. People who lack common-sense must perish, like those who revived the lion.'

'How was that?' asked the fourth of the friends.

And the stranger began:

'Once upon a time there were four wise men. Three of them were very book-wise, the fourth had, in addition, good judgment and common-sense. One day they all went for a walk and came upon the sun-bleached bones of an animal. The first of them said: 'Now we can prove our knowledge and skill. I know how to put these bones together.' And he put them together. The second one said: 'I know how to put on the flesh, the tendons, the blood and the skin.' And he did so. The third one said: 'I know how to bring the animal back to life.' At this the fourth one, who had noticed that the animal was a lion, cried: 'Wait a moment, until I climb up this tree!' When he was at the top, the third wise man revived the lion — and it devoured all three of them. Then, when the lion ran away, the fourth wise man climbed down the tree and went home. That's why I say that knowledge without common-sense leads to destruction.'

Tales Told by the Wanderer in Vada

Groaning with pain, the wretched hunter of pearls and precious stones whispered: 'Yes, I see you are right. I really lost my common-sense and good judgment.'

The stranger then went away, and the wheel spun round and round...

The wandering story-teller came to the end of his story. The listeners from Vada strolled home in groups, in a lively discussion of what they had just heard. That night Jagannath slept in the hut where the two boys sold sugar-cane syrup during the day.

In the morning he bought some food and juicy fruit, and left Vada. All the villagers he met on the way wished him a pleasant journey, and said they hoped he would come back again soon.

On the other side of Vada the jungle was a little less dense, but after he had walked a few miles, Jagannath found himself in the shadow of the rich foliage again, accompanied by the twitter and croaking of many kinds of birds, the buzz of bees, bumble-bees and all sorts of insects, and the shrieking of monkeys.

By the evening he arrived at Bhovargiri and immediately visited the house of his friend Ramratan, who was the headmaster, teacher and school porter of the local one-class school. There he washed off his weariness in cold water, dined with the family and later in the evening, when everone had finished his work, he sat down on the village green in front of the school amidst the old and the young, and began his story.

Minakshi, the Princess of the Lake

Legend has it that in ancient times the Sambhar Lake, which lies close to Jaipur, was inhabited by people like us. They had their kingdom there, and they behaved and lived under water the same way as people on dry land do. It is said that they also spoke the same language but that they could, whenever they wished, turn into fish.

Their king and ruler at that time had two children. The son was called Minakar and the daughter Minakshi. The king of the Sambhar Lake did not like people who lived on dry land, and therefore he did not allow his children, or any of his subjects, to visit the shores.

When Princess Minakshi reached the age at which it is suitable for young ladies to be married, she went to see her father and said to him: 'My dear royal father, I am grown-up, and I think I ought to marry. Indeed, I would very much like to get married. All of my friends who grew up with me are married, some of them have children, only I am still single and alone. I can't go on like this. Allow me to choose a young man, or choose one for me, if you wish. But please do something about it.'

The king was lost in thought for a while. In his eyes Minakshi was still a little girl, but in the end he admitted that his daughter was right. He also realised that a princess royal could not marry any of his subjects, and as for the dry-land people, he felt a strong dislike and resentment for them. So he said to Minakshi: 'I have to think the matter over carefully. I will let you know my decision later.'

When Minakshi left he at once called his son Minakar, and said: 'My son, your sister Minakshi would like to get married. I want you to keep an eye on her and to guard her carefully until I find a suitable husband for her. I fear lest her strong yearning to be wedded leads her to do something foolish. Above all take heed never to let her go on shore among the dry-land people.'

Minakar promised his father to do so, but he found the task a bit dull. He did watch Minakshi for a few days, but then he preferred to go catching crabs with his friends.

That day Minakshi felt unusually bored. She decided to take a walk. She went out of the royal palace, through the garden, opened a little gate and headed for the shore. Walking through the lake lawns, groves and woods, she had almost reached the shore when she observed strange ornaments hanging on long lines: glittering hooks of all sizes, made of shells, and pinned on each of them was a little fish, a worm or an olive. Minakshi had never seen anything like it before, and she found it very pretty. She thought that the ornaments would look nice in her chamber, so she cut some of them off with a sharp shell and took them home.

But these were no mere ornaments. They were the baits the fishermen of king Jaidev of Jaipur had set for fish they meant to catch for the royal kitchen.

When the fishermen came to take their catch, they saw that some of the hooks were missing. They said to each other: 'There must have been some unusually large fish here, to tear off our hooks.' And when they returned to Jaipur they reported it to King Jaidev.

The king looked at the remnants of the fishing lines and said: 'It was no fish that tore the hooks off. Someone cut off the lines. A fine set of fishermen you are, to let someone cut off your hooks under your very noses!' And he laughed heartily.

The fishermen, feeling foolish, looked gloomy, but King Jaidev said: 'Never mind, we'll soon find out who it is that steals your hooks!'

He advised them to put new hooks on the lines the next day, but instead of bait to hang beads and glass bracelets on them. The fishermen did as the king told them. Then they watched the waters of the Sambhar Lake attentively to see what would happen.

That day also Prince Minakar spent his time catching crabs instead of keeping an eye on his sister, and Minakshi went for a walk in the lake again. When she came to the shore she saw the glittering hooks of carved shell on the lines again, and hanging on them were beads and glass bracelets. She had just cut off three of them, when the fishermen saw her through the clear water and set up a cry. Minakshi took fright and quickly ran home to the royal palace in the middle of the lake.

The fishermen returned to King Jaidev and told him what they had witnessed: 'A beautiful maiden came along the lake's ground and cut off the hooks with a sharp shell. When we began to shout, she was startled and fled. The maiden is so lovely that it can't be anyone but the daughter of the Sambhar king.'

King Jaidev was glad to hear the news and rewarded the fishermen generously. Then he tried to find a way of meeting the lake princess, but nothing occurred to him. He could not go under water, for without air he could not live. And he knew that the inhabitants of the Sambhar Lake never went ashore because their king had strictly forbidden it.

In the meantime the king of the Sambhar Lake had learned that his son Minakar, instead of watching his sister, was catching crabs with his friends, and that Princess Minakshi had been taking walks all over the lake right up to the shore, although he had forbidden it.

He was very angry and summoned his son and daughter. When they arrived, and well aware of their guilt, paid their respect to him, he said in a resolute and stern voice: 'I am not pleased with you, children. You are disobedient, and have been doing whatever entered your heads. I must therefore punish you. Minakar, for not guarding your sister, and permitting her to go to the shore where she was seen by dry-land people, I banish you from our lake-kingdom! Go to the dry lands to live among the people there, and never return!' Turning to Princess Minakshi the king said: 'And you, daughter, will stay in our palace and will not set your foot outside its bounds or gates even to the length of two eels. Tomorrow you shall be wedded to a husband of my choice!'

Minakar sadly submitted to his father's orders, whereas the princess was pleased, because she sincerely longed to have a husband. The prince said goodbye to all his relations and friends and left for dry land.

But the Sambhar king did not wish to marry his daughter to any of his subjects, nor did he want her to have a husband from the dry lands. So he decided to marry her to the statue of a young man which was made of pink marble, and was standing at the palace gate. And he did so that very day.

Princess Minakshi was at first happy to have a husband, however she soon realised that he was of no use. Her husband never said a word, let alone caressed her, kissed her or embraced her. The unfortunate Minakshi consoled herself: 'Better any husband than none.' But it did not make her any happier.

Prince Minakar had meanwhile walked out of the lake on shore and, being tired, he lay down in a boat under a spreading tree, and fell asleep. The night was warm and Minakar slept calmly until morning. He woke up to the birds' song and the warm sun's rays. Minakar experienced something he had never known before. With an unusual feeling in his soul he walked away from the shore.

On his way from the Sambhar Lake to Jaipur he saw people working in the fields, shepherds with herds of cows, sheep and goats, he saw pedlars, merchants, villages bustling with life as villages usually are when everybody is engaged in work. He was enjoying it all immensely, for it was much brighter, more colourful, lively and distinct than at home in their lake-kingdom. He walked on and on until he came to the square in front of the royal palace in Jaipur. There he paused and lingered for some time, because he did not know what to do or where to go. Just then the king's chief counsellor, who was looking out of the window, noticed him, and at once came out of the palace.

He went straight towards Minakar and addressed him: 'Welcome, stranger. I don't know where you come from, but it seems to me that you are not familiar with things here, and need some advice and help. Is my guess correct?'

Prince Minakar told him all about himself. King Jaidev's counsellor was a wise man of experience. He had often talked with the king about the strange kingdom at the bottom of the Sambhar Lake, and he knew that the king was very interested in it. When he learned that

Minakar was the son of the king of the lake, he took him straight to king Jaidev and presented him to the king.

King Jaidev was very glad to meet Minakar, and after talking to him for some time, and becoming acquainted with him, he invited him to stay at the royal palace. They became good friends.

Once, and it was intentional on the part of Jaidev, the name of Minakar's sister Minakshi was brought up in the conversation. Jaidev mentioned the incident with the cut-off fishermens' hooks, and Minakar said: 'That was the very reason why father was so angry. I should have been guarding my sister Minakshi to prevent her from wandering all over the lake and getting to the shore, but instead I went crab-catching with my friends. Minakshi brought your fishermen's hooks home, because she thought they were some peculiar ornaments. When our father learned of this he was very angry with us for being disobedient.'

'Would it be possible to bring your sister here to dry land?' asked the king.

'Not by force or guile,' replied Minakar. 'If any of us lake people were made to leave the lake by force or guile, we would die within three days. But if anyone comes of his own free will, he can live with you here for the rest of his life. But it must be his wish, and he must do so on his own.'

'My fishermen told me your sister is a very beautiful maiden,' said King Jaidev. 'I would like to meet her.'

'She really is beautiful,' admitted Minakar, 'but I don't know whether she would decide to leave the Sambhar Lake.' At this the king became pensive and sad. He longed for the lake princess Minakshi, and tried to think of a way of making her come out of the lake without using force. Although he tried very hard, he could not find a way.

Prince Minakar watched him for a while and then he said: 'Listen, Your Majesty, perhaps this would work. My father did not want to marry my sister Minakshi to any of his subjects, and he hates us dry-land people. So he married her to a statue which stood at the gate of our palace. That certainly cannot be a husband my sister would be content with or could particularly love. I suggest you summon some sculptors and have them make several marble statues. Each succeeding statue must be more handsome than the preceding one, and their looks must more and more resemble yours. I will then return secretly to the

lake and place the statues in the correct order from our palace garden to the shore of the lake.'

'Well, it is an interesting idea,' said King Jaidev pensively, 'but I still can't see what good it would be.'

Minakar continued: 'Just listen, Your Majesty. Minakshi will go for a walk in the garden and will see the first statue, which will be much more handsome than her husband. Being curious she will go close to it to take a good look at it, but from there she will see the next statue in the distance, which will be even better-looking. And so she will go from one statue to another, until she reaches the shore where she will see you, the most handsome of them all. Then Minakshi will come ashore and the rest will be up to your skill and wit.'

King Jaidev found the idea very much to his liking. He laughed happily and gave Minakar a friendly pat on the shoulder: 'Your advice is excellent, prince! Thank you for the brilliant idea!' He immediately summoned sculptors and ordered them to set to work. When the statues were finished, Minakar did as he had said. He placed all the statues in the correct order from the lake palace garden right up to the shore of the Sambhar Lake. No sooner had he placed the last statue on the water's edge, than Minakshi went for a walk to while away time and amuse herself a bit. As she walked through the garden she saw a statue that had never been there before. She ran to it and inspected it thoroughly: 'What a handsome young man this is! He is much nicer than my husband.' But as she was looking around, she saw another statue a little way off, and it was even better looking. Surprised, she hurried to have a good look at it. And so she went further and further from the lake palace, and came closer and closer to the shore, where King Jaidev was waiting for her.

When he saw Minakshi admiring the last statue, which Minakar had placed at the water's edge, he beckoned her with his hand and said: 'Welcome, Princess Minakshi!'

The princess had stepped ashore by now, and suprised to hear the stranger call her by her name she said softly: 'Hail, stranger. Who are you, that you know my name?'

'I am Jaidev, king of Jaipur,' said Jaidev. 'I am waiting for you here because I want to take you to my palace and marry you. Do you want me?'

Minakshi blushed, but since she could not lie she answered shyly but truthfully: 'Yes, because you are the most handsome of all the men I have ever seen.' And so King Jaidev took her by the hand and led her to his palace in Jaipur.

There another surprise was in store for Minakshi — her brother Minakar.

And then all they had to do was to prepare the wedding celebration. It was the most glorious wedding the people of Jaipur had ever witnessed and the festivities lasted eight weeks. So the princess of the lake, Minakshi, became the queen of Jaipur.

When the king of the lake learned that his daughter had left him and had married the king of Jaipur, Jaidev, he raged, and for a long time the waters of the Sambhar Lake stormed and billowed, rising in waves of an unseen height. But as he could do nothing about it, and deep in his heart was very fond of his children, in the end he accepted things as they were and became a frequent and honoured guest of the Jaipur court. In due time Prince Minakar also married a maiden from dry land. After the death of the king of Sambhar all of his subjects walked out of the lake on to the shore and stayed there. Since then no more people have dwelt in the Sambhar Lake.

A light breeze carried the many scents of blossoming trees, bushes, herbs and grasses from the surrounding jungle. The wandering story-teller picked up his iktar, played a little tune and sang:

'Though the story seems a lie
Truth is hidden from the eye.
What's a lie and what is true?
Make a guess, it's up to you.'
And he began another story.

How Ka-nam Became the Bride of the Sun-prince

Long ago in the distant past in a village high up in the Khasi Hills there lived a man and his wife. They had a daughter named Ka-nam, a sweet little girl. When she had learnt to speak and walk and had grown a bit, her mother did not allow her to leave the house, for she was afraid of someone bewitching her or even worse, kidnapping her. But the father said: 'She is a child like all other children and must be brought up as such. She will have to learn to work and help us make a living!'

So they did as the father wished, but the mother was still anxious.

And then one day it really happened! Ka-nam was drawing water from a well, when suddenly the tigress U-khla rushed from the jungle in giant leaps and, snatching little Ka-nam by the waist, carried her in her jaws to her den.

Ka-nam's mother who saw it from the window set up a cry and all the villagers took their weapons and at once followed the trail, hoping to save little Ka-nam. But in the dense undergrowth they soon lost track of the tigress, and when evening came, they had to return home empty-handed.

The tigress U-khla put Ka-nam in her den and looked after her as if she were her own kitten. She brought her the sweetest of the jungle fruit, the most tasty bits of meat, she bathed her in a pool in the woods, and when it was cold she covered the entrance to the den with her own body to keep the cold out.

Ka-nam grew up and became a beautiful young maiden.

It was then that the other tigers living in the jungle said to U-khla: 'Listen, U-khla, that girl of yours has grown nicely. When are you going to invite us to a feast? It's time we tasted a bit of tender white meat.'

U-khla did not speak her mind, she only whisked her tail angrily, and quickly returned to the den. She knew only too well what it all meant.

Ka-nam was just tidying up the den, and sweeping the floor. The tigress came running all out of breath and cried: 'Dear Ka-nam, we're in great trouble! My fellow tigers have a mind to eat you! I can't defend you against them all alone. We must get you out of here at once, before it is too late.'

Ka-nam, frightened, her eyes filled with tears, asked: 'Where am I to go? My parents must be dead by now, and anyway I'd be ashamed to return among people.'

'There is only one thing you can do, dear Ka-nam,' said the tigress U-khla. 'Go to the wizard U-hynroh, who lives as an enormous toad in the moorlands on the outskirts of our jungle, and ask him for help. I will come with you.'

And so they went. When they were about half-way, they heard the roar of many tigers behind them. U-khla whispered: 'We'll have to hurry. The tigers have found out that you are running away, and they want to catch you and eat you.'

They both ran as fast as their legs would carry them, but the roaring tigers were getting closer and closer. 'Dear Ka-nam,' said tigress U-khla sadly, 'we will have to say goodbye here. Run straight ahead until you come to the tallest tree at the edge of the jungle, then turn left. From there it is only a short way to the moorlands, where you will find the wizard U-hynroh. I'll wait here and detain the tigers. Take care of yourself and don't think badly of me.'

Ka-nam began to weep and refused to leave U-khla, but the tigress roared at her so severely, that the frightened Ka-nam quickly took her leave and ran.

U-khla sat down and resigning herself to fate, waited. When the tigers caught up with her they asked her where Ka-nam was. But the tigress refused to tell them, and the tigers, enraged to have been deprived of a tasty titbit, tore poor U-khla to pieces.

Meanwhile, Ka-nam had reached the edge of the jungle and on coming to the tallest tree she turned left. Not far from there she could see the wide moorlands covered with sparse grass and bull-rushes. The bubbles oozing from the mud filled the air with the stench of sulphurous vapours. Ka-nam broke off a bamboo stick and cautiously walked into the moor.

Far away in the middle of the marshes there was a large cave, and inside, sitting on a crystal boulder there was a huge toad, the most hideous creature anyone could imagine. This was the wizard U-hynroh.

Ka-nam, suppressing a feeling of horror and disgust, bowed to him.

The wizard U-hynroh croaked: 'Who are you, what do you want here?'

Ka-nam told him everything in detail and in the end she asked him for help.

'I will help you,' said U-hynroh in his toady voice. 'Stay with me here as my servant, and I will protect you from all danger.' He was looking forward to having a beautiful slave-girl.

'But you must wear this toad-skin, so that nobody recognizes you,' added U-hynroh. 'And never take it off, or you will be severely punished!'

What could poor Ka-nam do? She put on the horrible toad-skin and no one would have guessed that it hid the beautiful maiden from U-khla's den.

In this manner Ka-nam lived for some time in wizard U-hynroh's cave, but she was not happy there, and all the time she contemplated ways of getting away. She was determined to escape at all costs, and day by day her decision grew firmer.

Soon she found a friend in the moors. It was the wizard U-hynroh's great-great-granddaughter, a pretty little frog with nice warty skin. The unfortunate Ka-nam confided to her that she would like to run away from the moors, but that she did not know how or where to go, because if she returned to the jungle the tigers would most probably tear her up and devour her.

'It's not so difficult, if you don't get dizzy and are not afraid of heights,' laughed the great-great-granddaughter, who was sorry for the poor girl. 'I'll tell you what to do. There is a tall tree, growing on the

edge of the jungle. You must have noticed it on your way here. It is a magic tree, though it doesn't look it. If you climb to its top and pronounce the magic formula, the tree will grow and grow right up to the sky. Then you can get off and live in heaven.'

'What is the magic formula?' asked Ka-nam eagerly.

The great-great-granddaughter leaned forward towards her and said softly:

'Low the earth lies
Close are the skies
Grow tree, grow up
Until I say stop!'

Ka-nam thanked the good little frog, and having said goodbye to her, she ran from the moorlands in her old toad-skin. The great-great-granddaughter called after her: 'Good luck!'

Ka-nam easily climbed to the top of the magic tree, for she was driven by her wish to escape the ugly toad-wizard. When she reached the top she put her arms round the trunk, and holding it firmly so as not to fall down, she said softly:

'Low the earth lies
Close are the skies
Grow tree, grow up
Until I say stop!'

And at once the tree began to grow taller and taller, until it reached the sky. Then Ka-nam cried: 'Stop!' and let go of the tree, which immediately regained its original size. And Ka-nam was in heaven.

For a time she wandered round, looking for someone who would employ her, but none of heaven's inhabitants wanted the ugly toad. At last the Sun-queen, Ka-sngi took pity on her and allowed her to guard the gate of her palace. And there she let her stay in a small watch-house.

Ka-nam was happy to have escaped the wizard U-hynroh, and did her best to serve the Sun-queen well. She was no more afraid of the wizard and so often when she was alone, she would take off her toad-skin and look at herself in the mirror. Once as she was standing there, Ka-sngi's son, the Sun-prince, happened to be passing by and saw her. He was so overwhelmed by her beauty and charm that he immediately went and told his mother about it. The Sun-queen was doubtful of his words, and decided to find out the truth. And she did.

She saw that her son had not been mistaken, that it was not the work of his imagination. Ka-nam really was beautiful. And since she liked her very much, she wanted her to become her son's bride. Ka-nam was invited to the palace, and soon at a wonderful wedding ceremony she became the wife of the Sun-prince.

On the wedding night, when Ka-nam was asleep, the Sun-queen carefully took her toad-skin and secretly burnt it. From then on Ka-nam could never again look like an ugly toad. And as the beautiful lady she was, she lived with the prince happily ever after.

The toad-wizard U-hynroh was very angry when Ka-nam ran away from him, and when he learned that she had escaped to heaven and that the Sun-prince had married her, he was furious. His eyes bulged with rage until they almost fell out, he croaked the most terrible curses, he was foaming at the mouth, and all his warts discharged poison. He immediately climbed to the top of the magic tree and jumped to heaven, intending to get revenge and to devour the Sun-queen, Ka-sngi.

But the Sun-queen knew how to fight and defended herself valiantly with her sun-arrows. However the people on earth were very anxious about the fate of the Sun-queen, and in order to frighten the toad-wizard U-hynroh, they gathered in great crowds and made a deafening noise by beating drums, kettle-drums, cymbals and all the other percussion instruments they could find, as well as by shouting, screaming and yelling.

How Ka-nam Became the Bride of the Sun-prince

The wizard, being a coward, was intimidated by the terrible row. He let the Sun-queen go, and crawled back to his cave in the moors. But he was so vindictive that he could not stop thinking of punishing the Sun-queen. And so to this day, every now and then, when he remembers how the Sun-queen helped Ka-nam and burned her toad-skin, he forgets himself and starts climbing to heaven to devour her. But whenever this happens, all the people of the Khasi Hills gather in great crowds and make a big noise to frighten him, and save the Sun-queen.

True, all other people call this the eclipse of the sun, but only because they are not familiar with this story. Only the people who live in the north east, in the Khasi Hills, know the real truth.

All the listeners were surprised for, they said to each other, as far as they knew it was the evil demon Rahu who wanted to swallow the sun, but they agreed that perhaps in the Khasi language Rahu was U-hynroh. The wandering story-teller picked up his iktar, played a little tune and then he sang:

'Though the story seems a lie
Truth is hidden from the eye.
What's a lie and what is true?
Make a guess, it's up to you.'

And he began another story.

Tales Told by the Wanderer in Bhovargiri

The Castle under the Sea

Tamralipti, the city which lies on the shores of the East Sea, was once ruled by king Chandasen. The king had a young servant named Ratan. Although Ratan had been serving the king for many years he had never received any pay, and had to manage without money as best he could. In spite of this he was devoted to the king.

One day King Chandasen, accompanied by horsemen and beaters, went hunting. His servant Ratan ran in front of the hunters. They came to the wood, which was full of game and the hunt began. The king pursued a large boar with such zeal and concentration that he soon vanished from the other hunters' sight. Only the faithful Ratan followed him, regardless of his own hunger and thirst.

Then, in the dense jungle growth the king lost track of the boar and also of his way back. He was extremely tired and hungry. When he saw that his servant had followed him he got off his horse and asked him: 'Ratan, do you know the way back?'

'I do, Your Majesty,' answered Ratan courteously. 'But you should first rest a little.' And he went to a near-by stream and brought the king some water. Then he took three radishes from a knot in the edge of his gown, and offered two of them to the king. He tended to the king's horse and then sat down a little way off.

The king asked him: 'Where did you get the delicious radishes?'

'Your Majesty, I have been living on radishes ever since I have been your servant because I have never received any pay,' answered Ratan truthfully.

The king felt ashamed for having been so neglectful, and when they returned to the royal seat he rewarded Ratan richly for his faithfulness and devotion. However he still felt he had not paid his debt completely.

After some time King Chandasen commissioned his servant Ratan to visit the king of Ceylon and ask the hand of the princess. Ratan boarded the royal ship and set sail. When he had sailed about half the distance between the two kingdoms, suddenly a golden flagstaff with a multi-coloured flag emerged from the waves in front of the ship. At the same moment a violent storm broke out, and the ship began to sink.

Undaunted, Ratan drew his sword and jumped headlong into the foamy waters, next to the flagstaff. No sooner had he done so than the ship fell apart and all aboard were drowned. Only Ratan felt himself sinking into the depths of the sea, until all at once he found himself in a wonderful city with glittering gold palaces and blossoming trees and flowers. Ratan thought that he was either under a magic spell, or dreaming.

But just then, from a temple in the centre of the square came the most beautiful maiden he had ever seen. Her eyes were blue like water-lilies on a lake, her body was as slender as the stem of a flower, her smile resembled jasmine blossom. Accompanied by her servants she walked to the most magnificent palace of the undersea city.

Ratan felt his heart burn with love for the unknown beauty, and he followed her there. He passed through several chambers and passages and found himself in front of golden bars. Opening them, he entered a lovely park. There, resting on a couch, was the beautiful maiden.

Ratan bowed to her and said: 'Please forgive me, oh beauty, for entering your palace without your permission. I have had the misfortune to lose my king's ship in a storm, and by some strange chance I have found myself in this undersea city. Please forgive me my intrusion, oh lovely maiden who seem to be the goddess of good fortune and happiness.'

'Welcome Ratan! I know you. You are my guest,' said the maiden sweetly. 'Go and wash in the pool beneath the old orange tree. Then, if you like, we can have something to eat and drink together.'

How could Ratan refuse? Joyfully he plunged into the pool under the old orange tree — but what was this? Everything began to spin, and suddenly he was in Chandasen's royal garden in Tamralipti. The undersea city had vanished. He could not comprehend it and wandered through the garden in confusion until the courtiers noticed him and reported it to the king. Chandasen came to Ratan and asked: 'How did you get here, my friend? Didn't I send you to the king of Ceylon?'

The puzzled Ratan told the king all he had experienced.

'Well,' the king said to himself, 'the time has come for me to repay my faithful and devoted servant.' Then he said to Ratan: 'Don't despair. I will take a boat with you and we shall sail the same way across the sea. We'll see if we can't gain the beautiful maiden for you.'

The following day the king consigned the government of the kingdom to his counsellors and together with Ratan he boarded a small sail-boat. They sailed alone, Ratan steering, and the king watching the sea and trimming the sails. Somewhere midway on the sea Ratan cried: 'Watch out, Your Majesty! Here comes the flagstaff!'

And indeed! A golden flagstaff with a multi-coloured flag emerged from the sea. At the same time a terrible storm broke out and Ratan shouted: 'Jump into the sea with me, Your Majesty!'

They both plunged fearlessly into the sea and soon they sank to the undersea city. When they came to the square with its magnificent temple, a beautiful maiden walked out of it, accompanied by a throng of girl-servants. King Chandasen had to admit that he had never seen a lovelier maiden. She had also noticed King Chandasen, and sent one of her servants to ask who he was.

The servant bowed to the king and Ratan, and invited them both to visit her mistress. 'Thank you,' answered the king, 'but we are not common men to obtrude on someone. Leave us alone.'

When the disappointed servant left, Ratan turned to the king: 'But sir, why did you not accept the invitation?'

'Don't worry, my friend,' said the king, 'you must never show your interest to a woman, or you will lose everything beforehand. Be patient and wait, for you will be happy in the end.'

And indeed! A moment later the beautiful maiden herself came, bowed low to them, and with her hands clasped before her brow invited them cordially to her palace. The king winked at Ratan so that the maiden would not see it, and hesitating a little, they accepted the invitation.

The maiden led them to an exquisite chamber, and treating them with great respect and honour, she said: 'I am the daughter of the ruler of the demi-gods. My father built this undersea city for me, but I am lonely here all the time without a husband.'

'Why don't you marry my friend Ratan?' said King Chandasen. 'He loves you and it was only because of you that he went to sea the second time.'

The lovely daughter of the king of the demi-gods bowed her head in consent.

And so Ratan became the ruler of the undersea city. King Chandasen stepped into the pool beneath the old orange tree, and returned to Tamralipti. However, before leaving he said to Ratan: 'I have repayed you for one of your radishes, but I still am indebted to you for the other one.'

The listeners walked off home. Jagannath went with his friend Ramratan and his wife, for he was to spend the night at their house.

When they came to the little cottage, Ramratan's wife Lakshmi put all three children to bed, and meanwhile Grannie Meghna made some tea. The children fell asleep at once, Grannie gave them all tea, and Lakshmi prepared some papar — fried lentil-flour chips in the little kitchen. When they finished their tea and crunched all the chips up, they all went to bed. In the morning the wandering story-teller said goodbye to Ramratan and his family, and continued his never-ending journey across the Indian countryside, where there is never a lack of exciting scents and odours, sweet and foul. For India is a wast country, colourful and fertile. In India you can find that which you will not see anywhere else in the world. And there is no sense in looking for something you cannot find in India anywhere else, for it does not exist. Such is India.

Jagannath walked up the winding path leading from Bhovargiri to Bhimashankar. He arrived there before sunset.

When he came to the empty courtyard of the largest of Bhimashankar's temples, he halted. The dark grey stone temple, its turnip-headed dome adorned with splendid reliefs, rose in the purple sunset glow. The entrance was pitch-black.

Jagannath walked past it, and was greeted by the children of Bhimashankar. Soon their merry voices attracted the citizens of the shrine town.

Jagannath refreshed himself by washing and eating a meal. Meanwhile the people gathered in the courtyard of the largest temple, and Jagannath began his story.

The Pearl Diver

This happened ages ago, when the mountains on our Earth were much higher, the rivers much longer, the seas much deeper, the forests far greener, the flowers were more colourful and the rice was much whiter. Today we know of those times only by word of mouth, because not even our oldest great-grandmothers or great-grandfathers remember them.

In those days on the shore of the east coast there was a fishing village called Machlipur, and in it lived a boy with his mother. The boy's name was Moti — pearl. He had earned himself this name because instead of going to sea on boats to catch fish with nets and rods like the rest of the men and boys, he dived into the waves from high cliffs, and looked for pearl-oysters. No diver in the village could match him. But though Moti found a pearl once in a while, he and his mother were very poor, for Moti could not sell pearls to the villagers who were as poor as he was. Once in several months a merchant from the city came on his buffalo cart, but he claimed that pearls were almost worthless as no one was interested in buying them, and always gave Moti only a few copper coins for them. And so they had to rely on their little rice field for a living. It yielded just enough rice to keep them alive.

One day Moti set out alone along the seashore for the distant Black Bay because he thought there might be more pearl-oysters there. The city merchant was to arrive soon and Moti wanted to have as many pearls as possible for him so that he could provide his mother with more money.

The bay had been named black because the coast was lined by rugged black cliffs which made the sea look black too. But the water was so clear that you could see through it to the bottom. Moti saw at once that there were many pearl-oysters there, but he also noticed a shoal of large sharks swimming in the bay. He stood there looking at the water for some time, but he did not dare to dive. He was an excellent swimmer, but sharks are faster than men, and Moti was well aware of that.

He returned home absorbed in thought, and told his mother that there were many pearl-oysters in the Black Bay, but also many sharks, so that he would have to find a way of getting at the oysters without risking too much.

His mother, feeling very anxious, said to Moti: 'My dearest son, please give up the pearls in the Black Bay. Sharks are not to be trifled with. We have enough rice, and once in a while we can get a fish, so what else do we need? Don't give me cause to worry; you are all I have.'

'I am fed up with dry rice,' replied Moti seriously. 'And since I get so little money from the merchant for each pearl, I must get more pearls in order to earn more money. Don't worry, mother, I won't let the sharks eat me. But I must get those pearls from the bay!'

What could his poor mother do? Moti had always been a stubborn boy and so she wept a little, hoping that Moti would not do anything foolish, but that he would outwit the sharks somehow.

The next day early in the morning Moti went to the Black Bay again. He sat down on the tallest cliff and watched the waves. Deep down at the bottom there were ten large sharks rolling about lazily in the water, among them the biggest one, their leader, Makar.

Moti knew that sharks never slept even when they were just floating, and that they would rush at any prey they saw or sensed. And since in those days all living creatures still spoke the same language, Moti said loudly so that the sharks could hear him: 'What a lot of pearl-oysters there are here! I'll dive for some. All the sharks are asleep but even if they were to wake up when I plunge into the sea, nothing would happen to me. For I gave the shark with the thinnest tail a banana yesterday, and he told me a trick by which I can fool not only ordinary sharks, but also that numskull Makar, for he is so stupid that I don't have to fear him in the least.'

And he pretended to be getting ready to jump into the Black Bay. Makar said to the other sharks with a sneer: 'Watch out, at least one of us is going to get a nice tit-bit. That boy won't be as salty as fish! As soon as he jumps, let's get him!'

But Moti picked up a large stone and threw it in the bay. The sharks all hurried to the place where they heard the splash. Moti meanwhile quietly dived into the water, quickly collected some pearl-oysters, and in the twinkling of an eye was back on shore.

When Makar saw him sitting on the rock, taking pearls out of the oysters, he gnashed his teeth and exclaimed: 'Damn! That boy got away!' And he remembered what Moti had said. 'There is a traitor among us! Let's see which of us has the thinnest tail!'

He lined up all the sharks and carefully inspected their tails. The sharks were quite calm, because they all had a clear conscience. Suddenly Makar pointed at the smallest one, who really had the thinnest tail: 'That's the traitor! That's him!' And before the poor wretch could move a fin, they all pounced on him and devoured him.

Moti picked up his pearls and returned home content. The next day he went to the Black Bay again. When he saw nine sharks with their leader Makar lying in the water, he said loudly: 'Today I will dive for some more pearl-oysters, but I shall not do it the same way as yesterday, because yesterday I gave some oranges to the shark with the biggest belly, and he told me how to fool ordinary sharks, and also that numskull Makar, who is so stupid that I need not fear him in the least!'

Tales Told by the Wanderer in Bhimashankar

And again he took a large stone and threw it far out in the sea. All the sharks darted to the place where they heard the splash, and Moti quickly dived under water, collected a few pearl-oysters and immediately returned to the shore.

When Makar found that Moti had fooled them a second time he boiled with rage. 'Which of you scoundrels has the biggest belly? Which of you betrayed us?' The sharks looked at each other uneasily, because none of them felt guilty, but nevertheless they all tried to pull in their bellies and to look as slim as possible. The most daring of them remarked: 'But Makar, you have the biggest belly! You are the fattest of us!'

No sooner had he said it than the furious Makar pounced on him and bit him in two. Then all of them devoured him.

And so Moti came for pearls every day. The shoal of sharks became smaller and smaller. They gradually ate the shark with a spot on his back, then the one with two missing front teeth, the one with a torn fin, and so on, until there was only Makar left in the bay.

And he was the strongest shark in the world, because he had the strength of all the sharks who had gradually eaten each other, until the last one was devoured by Makar. 'Now that I have got rid of all the traitors who had helped the boy by advice or deed, I am sure to succeed. The boy can't fool me any more. At last I will have my tit-bit.'

But Moti was so sure of himself by now that he decided to bamboozle Makar. He took two sticks with pointed ends, two sticks for kindling fire, some dry cow pat to burn, a sharp shell and a little salt. Standing on the edge of the cliffs above the Black Bay he said loudly so that Makar would hear him well: 'I don't have to play any tricks today, because only the old numskull Makar is left here. But even if he caught me and bit me in two nothing would happen to me, for as soon as my blood appeared on the surface, my mother would come and revive me with magic. But if Makar were to swallow me whole, that would be the end of me!' And he dived into the sea.

Makar, who had heard him, dashed at him and gulped Moti down with all he held in his hands as if he were a tiny fish.

But before he could shut his jaws, Moti put two pointed sticks across them, and he had to leave them open. Then Moti made a fire in the shark's belly, scraped some tasty bits of meat off his ribs with the sharp shell, roasted them, put salt on them and ate them.

Poor Makar cried with pain, dashed from one end of the bay to the other, dived to the bottom, jumped above the surface, hit about with his tail, but all in vain.

Then Moti said loudly to make sure the shark would hear him: 'As long as Makar stays in the sea I am safe. But should he swim to the sandbanks of our village Machlipur, I'm lost.'

Makar thought: 'That's it! I'll swim to the shallowest sandbank and kill you, you rascal!' And as fast as he could he swam to Machlipur. Heading for the sandbank at a great speed, he ran aground almost on the shore and got stuck among the stones and seaweeds.

The fishermen crowded around the huge shark and beat Makar to death. Then they began to talk of skinning and disembowelling him. Moti called from the shark's belly: 'Cut carefully, because I, Moti, am inside.'

What a surprise it was for everyone when Moti crawled out of the shark's belly! He became the hero of the village, and had to tell everybody how he first fooled all the sharks in the Black Bay, and in the end even their leader, Makar. Everyone was amazed and praised Moti for his courage and cleverness, only his mother wept silently when she imagined all that could have happened to her son.

A few days later the city merchant came on his buffalo cart to Machlipur. Moti offered him all the pearls he had found in the Black Bay, and it was quite a bagful. One of the pearls was unusually large and beautifully pink. Moti had found it the very first day, when he had fooled the sharks for the first time.

The merchant gave Moti the usual few copper coins for each pearl. But Moti saved the large pink pearl for the end and said, showing it to the merchant: 'How much will you give me for this one? I have never seen one like it before, it must be very precious.'

The merchant's little pig-eyes gleamed greedily, but he immediately regained composure and mumbled indifferently: 'This one? It's not worth a single copper coin. Jewels are made of white pearls only. A pink one would spoil the effect. But as you have supplied me with pearls for such a long time, I will give you two copper coins for it.' And he looked forward to making a great profit by selling it to the king in the capital city.

Moti was disappointed, but something told him not to trust the crafty merchant. So he took the pink pearl back, and said: 'Well, that is really bad luck. If it is not worth a single copper coin I'll keep it as a souvenir of how I fooled the sharks in the Black Bay.'

The merchant immediately offered him three copper coins for it, but Moti did not change his mind. The merchant's persistence only confirmed his suspicion.

When the merchant left for the royal court, where he intended to sell the pearls at more than a hundred times the price he had given Moti, the boy wrapped the pink pearl in a silk scarf and set out for the capital city.

He easily found the royal palace. When the guards stopped him, he said: 'I have brought the king something I found in the Black Bay.' But he did not tell them what it was.

Once in front of the king, he knelt by the throne and spread the silk scarf out on the carpet. The large pink pearl shone like the most precious diamond.

'Where did you get the most beautiful pearl I have ever seen?' asked the king gently.

And Moti told him how he dived for pearls in the Black Bay, how he fooled the sharks and killed their leader Makar, how the merchant paid him a few copper coins for white pearls and had offered him two for the pink one.

'And as this pink pearl is the largest and the loveliest I have ever found,' concluded Moti, 'I have brought it as a gift for you.'

The king was very pleased with that. He summoned his chief counsellor and gave him two orders. The first was to send two guards for the pearl merchant and have them punish him in the courtyard by a hundred and eight cane strokes on his soles, the second — to pay Moti a hundred and eight gold coins from the treasury. Then he bade Moti farewell and reminded him to bring all the pearls he found directly to him, for he would pay Moti the price they were worth.

Moti, a wealthy man now, returned home to his mother in Machlipur with a bag of gold coins, and they lived together happily. After some time Moti married well, but he did not give up pearl-diving. And he became famous for the pearls he found, not only on the east coast, but also far inland.

All had liked the story and showed their approval by shouting: 'Vah, vah!' The wandering story-teller picked up his iktar and played a little tune. Then he sang:

    'Though the story seems a lie
    Truth is hidden from the eye.
    What's a lie and what is true?
    Make a guess, it's up to you.'

And he began another story.

How Jasvant, King of Gujarat, Overcame the Goddess of Fate

Once upon a time the land of Gujarat was ruled by the kind and wise King Jasvant, who was more concerned with the welfare and happiness of his subjects, than with his own peace and comfort. Very often he would go in disguise among his people in order to see for himself how they lived and how they were faring. And whenever he came upon poverty or ill fortune, he did all he could to help.

One day he came to a little village, and as it was evening, he asked the mayor to take him in for the night.

The mayor and his wife received the guest cordially, treated him to a tasty dinner, and then they all went to bed. That night the mayor's wife gave birth to a son.

They all fell asleep again, except for the king, who as he lay awake suddenly saw a woman of sublime beauty appear at the cradle. She held a jar with kumkum ink and a reed pen with a pearl-studded holder in her hand. The godly woman took the little boy's hand and began to draw some lines on the palm. These were the lines of his destiny. She carefully drew one line after another, but as she was drawing the line of life, her pen broke and the line remained unfinished.

The woman looked dismayed and was about to leave, but King Jasvant sprang up and said: 'Who are you, an apparition, or a human being?'

'Let me leave, King,' answered the woman softly. 'I am Vidhatri, the goddess of fate. I came to draw the mayor's son his lines of destiny, but as I was drawing his line of life, my pen broke.'

King Jasvant asked: 'What does that mean?'

'It means,' replied the goddess, 'that he will die young. And it will happen when he reaches the age of eighteen, while he is walking round the sacred fire with his bride. Then a terrible lion will attack him and kill him.' And the goddess of fate vanished.

The king pondered about it and said to himself: 'I must not allow this to happen. Since I am warned beforehand, I must do all I can to prevent it.' He did not sleep for the rest of the night. At dawn he said goodbye to the mayor and his wife, paid them well for the board and lodging, and before leaving he said: 'I am your King, Jasvant. You did not know this. Nevertheless you treated me kindly and were very hospitable to me. I would like you to do one thing. Please invite me to the wedding of the son who was born tonight. I beg you not to forget.' The mayor and his wife promised to do so, and they really kept their promise.

Eighteen years later the mayor's son was having a glorious wedding, and a splendid royal procession was approaching the village. King Jasvant, riding a huge white elephant, was surrounded by his courtiers on superb black horses, and by soldiers on brown horses. He was greeted by the sounds of drums, trumpets and horns, and all the villagers assembled to bow to their King Jasvant.

In front of the mayor's house the king dismounted from the elephant, hailed the wedding guests, and gave the bride and the groom his royal gift — a beautiful chest, inlaid with eight precious metals, and full of gold coins.

The courtiers and the soldiers had their orders, and they immediately surrounded the whole village, forming a human chain around it to prevent anyone entering. That is how King Jasvant wanted to oppose Fate.

The wedding ceremony began. The village priest gave his opening speech and the groom took the bride by her hand, and together they commenced walking around the sacred fire, their right side turned towards it. Everyone watched in silence, and King Jasvant, holding his mighty sword, looked round warily, lest the lion, which the goddess of fate had spoken of eighteen years ago, should appear. He could see nothing disturbing. The bride and the groom had almost completed the circle round the sacred fire.

Suddenly the terrible roar of a lion sounded, and from a shelf on which a clay jug with various animals painted on it was standing, leaped a lion. The enormous animal pounced on the groom, bit through the artery on his neck, and returned to its place on the jug standing on the shelf. Nobody could do anything. The lion's attack was so sudden and unexpected, that even King Jasvant was unable to use his sword.

The wedding ended abruptly in great distress. The priest went to the temple to sacrifice to the gods, the wedding guests left sadly.

King Jasvant begged the mayor and his wife to permit him to take their son's dead body to the capital. He said: 'Although I could not save your son from death however hard I tried, I will not give up trying to bring him back to life.'

The mayor and his wife gave him permission, because they were so overwhelmed by the sudden strange death of their son, that they completely forgot that according to the holy writ they should arrange the funeral rites. And so King Jasvant took their son's body to his palace in the royal seat.

There he had it laid on a marble bed in a cool vault, and anointed with scented balms. Then he consulted reputed doctors and herbalists but no one knew how to revive a man who had been killed by a lion.

The king decided to go and seek healing roots and herbs himself. He wandered through the woods and jungles, picking all unusual plants he came upon, and then he tried their five parts; the roots, leaves, flowers, fruit, and the rind. But it was no use. The mayor's son remained dead.

After many weeks, when the king was once again looking for herbs and roots in the forest, he suddenly saw a large fire burning in the distance. He hurried there and heard a human voice crying from the fire: 'King Jasvant, King Jasvant, save me from the fire or I'll burn to death!'

Without hesitation King Jasvant jumped into the blaze and saw a coiled cobra lying there. He quickly grasped it and carried it out of the fire.

The cobra said to him: 'Thank you, King Jasvant! You have freed me from the fire which I was doomed to by the saint Narad, for having offended him unwittingly. Without your help I would have suffered here in the flames for ever.'

'Don't thank me, snake,' said King Jasvant. 'I was glad to help you in your distress. I would do it again any time, if need be.'

The cobra rejoined: 'I would like to show you my gratitude. How can I help you?'

'I personally don't need any help, dear snake,' answered King Jasvant, 'but perhaps you could help a young man who was destined to die. I would like to revive him and return him to his bride and parents.'

The cobra looked the king straight in the eyes and said: 'Come with me to my nest, I will give you something.' And it crawled in front of the king deeper into the forest. When they arrived at the nest the cobra told the king to wait a little. It wriggled down into the nest, and instantly was back with a little earthenware bottle.

'Take this bottle,' it said. 'It is the nectar of the King of Snakes, which my grandfather once got from the king of all snakes, reptiles and lizards. Put a few drops on the dead man's lips, and he will come to life.'

King Jasvant took the bottle gratefully, said goodbye to the cobra, and hurried back to the castle. In the marble vault he put a few drops on the lips of the mayor's dead son, and immediately the young man shuddered, opened his eyes and said softly: 'Where am I? What happened to me?'

'Everything is all right now, my boy; you are alive again,' said the smiling King Jasvant. And at that moment the goddess of fate, Vidhatri, appeared and said: 'King Jasvant, you have overcome Fate! No mortal has ever succeeded in doing this before, you brave, persevering king! May you live a long and happy life, for only he who does not succumb to fate, but fights it, is worthy of living in this world.' And with this she disappeared.

Then King Jasvant took the revived man back to the village to his bride and parents, and the wedding could at last be concluded. And it was such a splendid wedding that all Gujarat talked of it long afterwards.

Somewhere close by an owl hooted. The wandering story-teller picked
up his iktar and played a little tune. Then he sang:
    'Though the story seems a lie
    Truth is hidden from the eye.
    What's a lie and what is true?
    Make a guess, it's up to you.'
And he began another story.

The Inheritance

In a village near Peshavar there lived an old shepherd. He had seventeen camels and three sons. The eldest son's name was Husain, the second son's name was Hasan, and the youngest one's was Hasin.

One evening when they were all having a plain dinner the father said: 'My dear sons, I am pleased with you, for you are taking good care of our camels and we need not fear poverty or hunger. But I am afraid that when I die, and that may be soon, you will become selfish and begin to quarrel.'

Husain and the other sons assured their father that this would never happen, that they would go on looking after the camels together, but their old father shook his head: 'Oh no, I have known you all since you were babies, and I know human nature. But I want to prevent you from quarrelling, and have therefore decided that when I die you are to divide the camels between you this way: the eldest, Husain, will get half the herd, the second, Hasan, will get a third, and the youngest, Hasin, a ninth. Don't forget, when I die, each of you take your share, and fare well.'

The sons promised their father to do as he wished and they all went to bed. In the morning they found that their father had died during the night.

After the funeral the sons got down to dividing the inheritance, but somehow they were unable to work it out.

The eldest, Husain, said: 'Father bequeathed me half the camels.

But half of seventeen is eight and a half. How can I take half a camel? Let's round it off and I'll take nine.'

'Oh no, you won't!' cried Hasan. 'That would not be fair. You already have the largest share. Take eight of them, and Hasin and I will share the rest.'

But Husain objected: 'In that case you would cheat me of half a camel. Of course I am not so concerned about that, but we must obey our father's will!'

The youngest, Hasin, interrupted: 'How about selling that camel? Husain would get half the money and the other half could be divided in all fairness between Hasan and me.'

Hasan said: 'Never! It would be a pity to sell a camel! We are not selling anything!'

They went on arguing for a long time without coming to any conclusion. Then Hasin said: 'Let's do this: we'll kill one camel, give half of it to Husain and let him do whatever he wants with it, and use half for a feast to honour the memory of our father.'

Husain and Hasan both exclaimed: 'The boy has gone crazy! He wants to feed the whole village free of charge!'

Hasin tried to calm them down: 'Stop quarrelling, brothers! We must find a fair solution. I have and idea. Let's just divide the herd for the time being, and anyone who gets more than he should, will give the one who gets less one or two baby camels when they are born.'

At this both Husain and Hasan sprang up shouting: 'Nothing of the sort! What if the mother camel dies? You'd like to get a baby camel for nothing, wouldn't you? And what if the camels get a disease?'

Hasin did not know which way to turn and began to shout too: 'Then make a better suggestion.'

Just then a fakir, a holy man, was passing their cottage on an old camel and heard the commotion. He asked kindly: 'Why are you quarrelling, brothers? Don't you know that anger and discord makes the blood grow thick and is damaging to the liver?'

Hasin replied: 'We don't know how it happened, but we got into an argument, honourable old man.'

'You were here when it happened, weren't you?' said the fakir.

Husain said: 'Oh yes, but we did not mean to quarrel. It happened because we cannot divide the inheritance our father bequeathed us.'

And all three of them told the holy man how their father had left them seventeen camels, and how they were to divide them among themselves according to his wish, but were unable to reach an agreement.

'Well, brothers,' said the fakir, 'I will help you. Take this camel of mine, then divide the whole herd peacefully and stop quarrelling.'

'We couldn't do that. It's too kind of you!' exclaimed the brothers. 'How could we deprive you of your property?'

'Don't worry and take it. If Allah wills, I shall not be the poorer for it,' said the fakir smiling.

So the brothers took the fakir's camel, and now the herd numbered eighteen. They divided it according to their father's will: a half to the eldest, Husain — that was nine camels; a third to the second son, Hasan — that was six camels; and a ninth to the youngest — that was two camels.

And suddenly the brothers looked in amazement — the fakir's old camel was left over! They were speechless with surprise.

The fakir-holy man mounted his camel, made a friendly gesture with his hand and said: 'You see that there is no sense in quarrelling, and that it is best to settle things in a friendly manner.'

And he went his way.

It was late at night. The wandering story-teller picked up his iktar and played a little tune. Then he sang:

'Though the story seems a lie
Truth is hidden from the eye.
What's lie and what is true?
Make a guess, it's up to you.'

And he began another story.

The Punishment of the False Sage

A vagabond and his fellows settled in a small town in the Hariyana country. When the local people, who were curious, asked who he was and where he came from, he told them that he was a holy man and a sage, who had studied at all the famous universities, and that there was no one in the world to match him in wisdom. And that his companions were his disciples, and were therefore also very wise. Of course, none of this was true.

People believed him because they were credulous by nature, and because no one had ever lied in their town before.

The false sage announced that he was willing to hold discourse on any chosen subject with anyone. And he found some people who wished to try their wit, but the sage always imposed upon them, so that they were at a loss for arguments. According to rules he had set beforehand they then had to give him the things they had put to stake, which was never a small amount. The sage always suggested a large sum of money, or rice, butter, flour and other foodstuffs as the wager. And so the impostor and his companions led a very pleasant life without having to work.

The mayor of the town would have liked to take steps against him, but there was no law enabling him to do this. So he decided to participate in the discourse. The false sage greeted him courteously and asked: 'What subject would you like to discuss, sir?'

'Well, perhaps we should talk of things that are, and things that do not exist,' said the mayor.

'Very well, sir,' said the false sage. 'Tell me then, sir, does Mount Kailas exist?'

The mayor answered truthfully: 'It does.'

'Have you ever seen it?' demanded the false sage.

The mayor admitted sincerely: 'No, I have never seen it.'

'And do you know anyone who has seen it?' continued the impostor.

'No, I don't.'

And the impostor said: 'In that case Mount Kailas does not exist, and you have lost the wager!'

The mayor, taken aback, said: 'That's not true! Mount Kailas exists even though I have never seen it!'

But the impostor's alleged disciples started clamouring: 'He has lost! He has lost!'

The mayor was forced to give the sage the whole stake.

He was very upset about it. Not so much because he had lost, but because it had not been a fair discussion and the scoundrel had imposed upon him. He told his wife about it gloomily, and she said: 'You should have been more cautious. You know he is a cheat. But don't worry, we'll get him. Tomorrow I will go and discourse with him, and we'll see if I don't corner him.'

The mayor was a bit surprised that his wife dared to challenge a trickster as artful as this one, but on the other hand he knew very well that she was sharp-witted, and had a ready tongue.

The mayor's wife visited the false sage the very next morning and brought a few good friends with her.

'I want to discourse with you, sage,' she said without much ado. 'These are my disciples,' she said pointing to her friends, 'I am sure you will not object to their presence at the discussion, just as we do not object to the presence of your disciples.'

The false sage, willy-nilly, had to consent, and when they were all seated he asked eagerly: 'And what will the stakes be?'

'I am willing to wager all my property,' said the mayor's wife. 'And the only thing I want you to wager is a single hair from your thick beard. I'll be quite content with that.'

The false sage was amazed. 'How can you be content with something so worthless and trivial?' he demanded.

'It is not as worthless as you may think,' replied the mayor's wife. 'But instead of wasting time in idle talk let's start the discourse.'

The sage began: 'What do you want to discuss?'

'Let's talk about the almightiness of the eternal gods,' said the mayor's wife.

'Very well,' he agreed. 'Tell me your opinion on the subject.'

'The eternal gods,' declared the mayor's wife, 'are not almighty. That is only an assertion preached by the priests, because it is in their interest, and because they profit by it.'

The false sage laughed: 'You have lost, for the eternal gods are almighty and can accomplish anything they wish!'

Tales Told by the Wanderer in Bhimashankar

And his so-called disciples began to clamour, clapping their hands and shouting: 'She has lost! She has lost!'

'I have not lost at all!' the mayor's wife stopped them abruptly. 'Tell me, sage, whether the almighty gods can create a mountain so heavy that they could not carry it, or a sea so large that they could not swim across it, or an age so long that they could not outlive it?'

The false sage was silent, unable to swallow or spit, for he knew that whatever his answer he would confirm that the gods were not almighty.

The friends of the mayor's wife began to laugh and clapped their hands shouting: 'He has lost! He has lost!' And they hopped around dancing with joy.

The mayor's wife stood up and said: 'You have lost, sage! Give me a hair from your beard!' She went up to him and tore a hair off his beard.

'Every hair of this wise man is magic!' she cried. 'If you throw a single one into a bag where there are the last two or three grains of rice left, the bag will fill with rice and will stay full no matter how much rice you take from it. If you throw a single hair into a jar with the last drops of melted butter — ghi — the jar will fill with butter and will remain full, no matter how much butter you take from it. If you throw a single hair into a money-box where there are the last few coins left, if will fill with money and will stay full regardless of the amount of money you take from it. That is the magic of his beard, and the reason why I demanded a single hair as the stake!'

The false sage's companions stared in amazement. 'And you never told us a thing!' they said reproachfully. 'A nice friend you are! You ought to be ashamed of yourself!' And pouncing on him they began to pull the hair out of his beard.

The false sage attempted to defend himself, crying that it was not true, but all in vain. He was powerless against them. And when his companions had finished with him, the friends of the mayor's wife got hold of him and each of them wanted to pull out at least one of his hairs.

Soon the news spread through the town and people from all over the place rushed at the impostor, trying to get at the few remaining hairs of his beard.

The sage was desperate. Bare-chinned, he left town and retired to a distant place, and no one ever heard of him again.

The Punishment of the False Sage

The wandering story-teller, Jagannath, came to the end of his last story. The villagers of Bhimashankar went home laughing. Jagannath had already chosen a nice little wooden temple of Gorakhanth, with a cosy porch, and now he lay down to sleep there, because Bhimashankar was a little village, and the cottages were the smallest in the whole neighbourhood.

Early in the morning, as soon as the sun rose, Jagannath washed in the water tank and made some tea on the fire. The villagers were just setting about their everyday tasks.

Then he picked up his musical instrument, the iktar, and a small bundle containing all his belongings, and left Bhimashankar. The rainy season was about to begin, and Jagannath headed for home at Manchar.

In India the rainy season is a time when everyone returns home. The caravans end their long journeys, wandering monks retire to the monasteries, merchants and shopkeepers store up their goods and settle their accounts, the peacocks start strutting and craning their necks towards the cloudy heavens, full of the promise of life-renewing water, and the whole country waits for the rains to make the earth fertile and enable it to yield a new crop.

And Jagannath was also going home. But once the rainy season was over, which would be in just two months' time, he would set out again to wander through the villages and little towns, and entertain people with his stories, which though they may not be true, nevertheless contain the sweet almonds of eternal truth and deep wisdom.